CREDENCE

Skye McNeil

For information, contact the publisher, Hot Tree Publishing.

WWW.HOTTREEPUBLISHING.COM

EDITING: HOT TREE EDITING

COVER DESIGNER: BOOKSMITH DESIGN

FORMATTING: RMGraphX

E-book ISBN: 978-1-925853-80-3

Paperback ISBN: 978-1-925853-73-5

For Cameron.

PROLOGUE

Twilight skimmed over the Italian coast, lulling the occupants of the sleepy city. In another few hours, they would leave, never to visit again. Cameron Shearer rifled through the duffle bag beside him, the bars of gold of little interest to him. They weren't the reason he was in Italy.

A flutelike voice caught his attention. She was the reason, and a dastardly one at that. He crushed a piece of paper into a ball before tossing it toward the trash can on the other side of the room.

Bambina Del Rossi had dragged him halfway across the world to rob a mobster wannabe. Though they were a couple, Cameron was done with the way Bambi manipulated everyone to get her way. Naturally, most of the men in the Del Rossi mob did everything she wished—him included. It took him half the time than the rest of the mobsters to see through her charade. *But not fast enough.*

Cameron stood and opened the small window. The sweet smell of fresh bread drifted on the wind. Jerry Del Rossi wasn't aware of his sister's rampant ways, and the same could be said about the other two Del Rossi mob bosses. Bambi was the sweet and innocent type… until she wasn't.

It was why they were in Italy. Somehow, she got the two of them invited to a millionaire's house party, only to sneak into the man's personal safe and deplete it completely. She always had a reason for her madness; this one was that the man had shunned her years ago, and Bambi never forgave him. It was typical of the blonde bombshell. She held grudges until she had the opportunity to get even—and would she ever. He shivered. If he never saw the conniving Bambina Del Rossi again, it would be too soon. He was thoroughly done.

Unbuttoning the crisp, white shirt, Cameron caught sight of his reflection in the mirror across from the room. The tattooed moth on his left bicep made him forget his troubles for the moment. He didn't know exactly why he'd chosen to permanently ink the memory of a long-ago past, but it reminded him that somewhere in the world a sassy brunette was living the better end of the fairy tale they'd conjured as kids. He shook his head and scoffed. No doubt, that same girl had forgotten about him many years ago. Their paths would never cross again. He wasn't even sure if his life would extend beyond the next week.

It was time to spill all the details of what Bambi had been up to while using the Del Rossi name. Her brothers may kill him the instant he finished—he was an accomplice, after all, in funneling Del Rossi money from their accounts—but he couldn't keep living a lie. At least not one this big.

He was all for making money and eluding the authorities. He'd made a decent career out of heists, drugs, and fencing expensive gems while under Del Rossi tutelage. But over the years, he'd begun to yearn for more out of life. He didn't want people hurt, and that was precisely what Del Rossi had done ever since he was a child. Plus, Bambi was ruthless and out of control. He wanted something better in his life. A woman who'd be a partner, not the person barking orders and throwing him under the bus when it suited her.

Cameron looked over at the bounty he and Bambi had scored over the last few days. It was nothing compared to the riches hidden away in several spots across Europe. There was enough to make either of them disappear for a while. He'd give her a choice. She could either come clean to face her brothers' wrath or she could take an extended vacation and leave him the hell alone. He cleared his throat and let the black bow tie flutter to the floor. In the alternative, his soon-to-be ex-girlfriend might just kill him—or let her brothers do the dirty deed while she preened from the shadows.

Worst case, he died. Best case? He shrugged. There was no best-case scenario with the Del Rossi mob. There was either life or a half-life. *Unless I can figure a way out.* He shook his head at the idiotic notion. No one escaped the mob. *Just like no one gets their happily ever after.*

CHAPTER ONE

"Yo, Shearer, wake up!"

Sitting up fast, Cameron inhaled sharply and tried to catch his breath. He placed a hand over his heart and willed it to slow. *Damn dreams*. Ever since Bambi made her grand appearance the week before, tidbits of his past kept popping up when he dared to sleep. They weren't just dreams, though. Most of them were memories, and that made then ten times worse.

He'd taken extra shifts to keep them at bay, but the lack of sleep didn't help. In fact, it made the apparitions worse when he did close his eyes.

He pushed back his hair, mussed from sleep. A trickle of sweat raced down his muscular chest to the sculpted abs below. Swinging his legs over the side of the cot, he reached for his phone. Two messages from his fiancée, Joci Dorous, awaited him. If he could manage a smile, he would. But not yet. He didn't deserve any happiness while he stowed away the secrets of his past come back to haunt him.

"What the hell are you doing in there?" Quinn yelled from down the hall. "If I come in there, I better not see your pants down—"

"Shut it, Quinn," Cameron replied, chuckling. He knew precisely what his partner would say if he let him finish. "You know I save those occasions for when I'm with Joce. She likes to watch."

Quinn was suddenly in the doorway; his green eyes alight with humor. "Oh, yeah? Tell me more," he teased in a voice befitting a teenage girl.

Cameron smirked and pulled on a fresh T-shirt. "You're a little too eager to hear about Joci's and my sexcapades, Levi." He lifted his brows. "I think somebody needs to get laid."

"Never said I didn't." He nodded to the bed. "Have you been home lately? I swear I've had to wake you up at the station all week." He clucked his tongue. "Pretty sure Joci wouldn't approve."

"She doesn't, but she understands." Pulling on the rest of his police uniform, Cameron shrugged. "Bills come every month."

"Mm-hmm, sure." Quinn shook his head. "More like trying to get out of diaper duty."

"Nothing you wouldn't do either." He laced his shoes, patting his thighs once, and stood. "All right, let's get out there before someone else gets the good cases."

Tossing him a granola bar, Quinn grinned. "Don't worry, partner, I have just the thing you need. An attempted bank robbery. Delancey and Stevens responded first, but I bet they need a little backup by now. Those two are worse rookies than even you were."

"Thanks, asshole." Cameron grabbed his phone and reminded himself to call Joci later. He really needed to go home. The only thing keeping him away was Bambi Del Rossi. If he stepped into their house and saw Joci with a baby on each hip—which was incredibly sexy, in his opinion— he'd spill every last detail about his ex-girlfriend and why she was in town. As tempting as baring his conscience sounded, Joci already had enough on her plate. He'd tell her. *When the timing is right.*

He followed Quinn through the station, the two stopping every now and then to chat with fellow officers and a few sergeants, then to get fresh coffee. Once they reached the front, he fished out the keys and climbed into the new SUV he and Quinn had been assigned.

Starting the vehicle, he let Quinn take over the radio, giving dispatch their route. Cameron guided the sleek SUV to the street and crossed into traffic. The courthouse loomed in the distance, reminding him of Joci. He needed to talk to his fiancée nearly as badly as he needed to kiss her.

But first, he had to get through this shift. She'd be all his for the weekend. Her best friend, Rayna Alley, had offered to watch their twin boys on Saturday, and he'd jumped at the thoughtful suggestion. They had plenty of plans for the one day of childless time. If they made it out of the bedroom at all, he'd tell her about his wicked ex.

***

Ignoring Adrian Petosa had been nearly impossible two years ago, and the new version of the redheaded attorney wasn't much better. Joci Dorous tapped her pen on the oak table, waiting for the judge to arrive for their hearing. Beside her sat their client for that afternoon's status conference. The blonde wasn't the issue. Being a rich housewife who allegedly murdered her lover, one might think they were in danger, but the only menace in the room was the man sitting to Joci's right.

Her ex-husband, father of one of her sons, and equal partner at Petosa Law had been every inch a gentleman since his unexpected arrival last week. He wooed the courtroom as efficiently as the boardroom of the law firm down the street. Her law firm. She clicked the pen. *Our law firm.* At least until she somehow got out of it. The details still needed ironing out, since the board wasn't about to let any owner cut and bail, her included.

"Joce, you're going to have to talk to me eventually," Adrian leaned over and said under his breath.

Joci scribbled a note about preparing for depositions in the case and kept her gaze on the court reporter. The woman twirling her red ringlets hadn't stopped staring curiously at Adrian since they arrived. Joci couldn't blame her. She'd do the same if the circumstances were different. He was quite the eye candy, even with a scar on his cheek and matching ones beneath his expensive suit.

"I do talk to you," she responded with a polite smile. Even looking at him was avoided at all costs. She wasn't sure how she'd respond if forced to interact with Adrian more than they already did.

"No, you talk through me." He laid a hand on her arm, pausing her pen. "I don't care all that much, honestly." His words made her head come up.

Adrian smirked, the act too attractive to deny. "Thought that might get your attention. You don't like to be ignored."

Joci set her jaw. He knew her too well. "Fine. What do you want to discuss? Maybe where you've been these last months or why you joined a," she lowered her voice, "mob."

Adrian flipped through the pleadings in the red folder on the desk. "Always right to the point. It's one of the things I love about you."

"Adrian—"

"Sorry, time and place and all that." His blue eyes met hers, and she held her breath at the intensity. They spoke so many volumes of anguish and acceptance that she couldn't form a sentence.

Joci parted her lips, but Judge Hiller chose that moment to enter. She'd get her say in; she always did. *But not until later.*

She quietly listened to the county attorney and Adrian argue the facts of the case. She had to admit, Adrian was still on point when it came to the law. It was almost as if he'd never left. The tumultuous way he came in and out of her life still hadn't been fully explained. He had secrets, and she desperately needed to hear them for their young son's sake. The problem was, she didn't trust Adrian.

By the time the hearing ended, Joci had never been happier to head to the next one alone. Petosa Law demanded she and

Adrian take this case together to quiet the rumblings of the current clients. Evidently, not everyone was accepting of the story Adrian gave upon arrival. Hiding from a nefarious mob and faking his own death to get rid of them would do the same to her if she didn't know the truth.

"Joci, can you get the subpoenas ready for the Wiggins case?" Adrian caught up with her despite her speedy departure from the courtroom. "I'll make sure the court reporter is there."

Joci shifted her briefcase to her left hand. "Yeah, sure, no problem." She dug her phone out of her jacket pocket and sent an email reminder to herself.

She was only five steps away from him when his voice stopped her.

"I want to see him. Brett." His voice softened slightly, as if the request was sure to be denied. "I want to see my son."

Looking over her shoulder, Joci took in his wary eyes and nodded. "Of course. I'd never keep him from you, Adrian." She stepped down the first stair and heard him gain on her. *I knew these heels were a mistake today.*

"Thanks." He walked down in sync with her, glancing over every other step. "I'd really like to get together and talk. All of us."

She paused on the landing between staircases. "Do you honestly think we can just be friendly again?" She let loose the hostility she'd held back for what felt like years, when in reality it had just been a few days. "You abandoned us, Adrian." Her hazel eyes flashed. "Brett doesn't deserve that. He'll get used to you being around, and if you leave, he'll lose you all over again. We all would."

Adrian moved out of the way of the courthouse traffic. "It won't happen ever, I swear."

Joci took a cleansing breath and studied the sight in front of her. Even though she saw him almost every day, she wasn't sure if she'd get used to his new look. The jagged scar on his cheek made the preppy guy she met all those years ago seem like a distant memory. The gray designer suit molded to him in a new way, and she couldn't keep from staring at the dark blue shirt underneath the gray pinstripe tie.

She knew what lay beneath the thousand-dollar outfit. She'd seen the scarred flesh. The story behind it remained hazy. Trusting Adrian wouldn't come easy. She wasn't even sure she'd ever truly put her hope in him again. The last year had done a number on their relationship.

"I don't know what to believe when it comes to you," she said, looking him up and down.

"I deserve that." He straightened his tie and glanced to the bottom of the staircase. "I also deserve to be heard out."

"But—"

"Please, Joce." His blue eyes begged equally with the emotion in his voice. "You're an attorney. You know there's usually more to a client's story than what they tell us the first time." He held out a business card. "So let me tell you my story, and I'll let you come to a verdict."

Taking the offering, Joci waited until Adrian moved to the steps and started down without her before she read the card. It was for a therapist. The same one they went to years ago during their marriage. *He has some nerve….* She stopped herself there. Adrian had mentioned he'd seen a slew of doctors over the last six months. It made sense to include a shrink after all he'd been through. This particular one knew his history too.

Her gaze latched on to the man now at the bottom of the stairs. Adrian conversed with a fellow attorney, careful to keep his left side turned away. The scar wasn't horrible, if she were honest with herself. It was the story behind it she didn't want to face. The possibility that Adrian had indeed been an unknowing pawn gave her pause about her feelings for him. While she'd never love him in the same way, they'd always be connected.

She tucked the card in her pocket and continued on to her next hearing. She'd deal with Adrian later. For now, she had a busy day at court, then a weekend ahead with her favorite guys. She checked the time and groaned. Closing time was still too far off.

CHAPTER TWO

Snow peppered the top of Cameron's head, but he didn't bother to swipe it off. The entire world around him was blanketed in the fluffy stuff. It looked too pure for the setting. His brown eyes moved to where Jerry Del Rossi embraced his sister. Once upon a time, he'd been right next to Bambi at the Del Rossi dinner table. That ended rather quickly when he told the family about her unapproved methods of getting rid of witnesses and working through her vendettas. She may appear charming, but her viper tendencies had killed plenty of innocent people over the years. He didn't even want to think about her body count. It'd be staggering.

"Cameroni, come join us." Jerry waved one chubby hand at him.

Reluctantly, he shoved off the side of his black Jeep and walked over to where the small group of mobsters stood beneath the awning of the abandoned gas station on the outskirts of the city.

"Do you remember when we stole those gold bars from the Italian millionaire?" Bambi asked when he was close enough.

For a second, he merely stared at Bambi's bright red lipstick and large diamond stud earrings. How he'd ever loved her made no sense. He could only blame himself for wanting such a fake love. He'd tasted true love, and nothing else compared.

"Are you going to tell me how I get out of the mob now, or are we just going to rehash the past?" He cocked his head to the left, attention only on his boss. Avoiding Bambi from here on in was in everyone's best interests. "Because I have shit to do that's actually legal."

Jerry barked out a laugh, his bushy eyebrows seemingly gelled to match his slicked-back salt-and-pepper hair. "See, it's your candor that I respect so much, Shearer. Just when I think it'd be easier to simply snap your neck and feed you to hogs, you remind me why I like you." He toddled over and patted Cameron's shoulder in a fatherly fashion. "But no, we won't reminisce tonight." He glanced to his sister. "It probably wouldn't end well for you." He squeezed Cameron's bicep. "I have news of the drug shipment you and Bambi are to confiscate."

"I thought we were planning a jewelry heist." He cast a glance to the blonde Barbie wannabe who was reapplying her lipstick. He shuddered at the knowledge that smearing the unique red shade used to be his daily goal. "That's what Bambi and I do best." He cringed. *Did.*

One of Jerry's bodyguards handed him a folder. The enforcer opened it and pulled out a photo. "Don't worry, you'll do that too." He smiled to Bambi. "While my little sister was off in Asia, she managed to score some great connections with the drug runners there." He turned toward Cameron. "And you practically own the Midwest, thanks to our Mikkelsen debacle."

Cameron's blood cooled at the sound of Jerry's snicker. Following J.J. Jepsen's death, the Del Rossis had hunted down all Mikkelsen affiliates from New York to California. A few remained in the southern states, but with Del Rossi expanding there soon, most were fleeing back to their European haven. The Italians now worked hand-in-hand with the Central and South American cartels when it came to drugs.

"Oh, don't look so glum, Cameroni," Bambi crooned with a wide smile. He smothered the urge to wipe it right off her perfectly plastic jaw. The sound of his nickname on her lips was a knife to his back. "We'll do this job, then you'll be free to make more babbling babies with your attorney bimbo." She leaned close and gave him an air kiss. The scent of her Chanel perfume filled his nostrils, and he held back from gagging. "Simple as that."

Clenching his jaw, Cameron refrained from responding. It wouldn't do him any good. The three Del Rossi brothers would do anything their little sister asked. If she didn't enjoy the thrill of heists anymore, they'd probably give her a territory to run with her own miscreants. That idea sent a cold shiver down his spine. Bambi with unlimited Del Rossi power was a war waiting to erupt.

The last thing he needed was to get on her bad side even more than he already was. Bambi held grudges like it was her business. In a way, it was. Years ago, they'd stolen an expensive painting merely because the woman who owned it made fun of Bambi. "Petty" was the best word to describe Bambi.

"Who's the target?"

Bambi snatched the file. "Donald Wong." Her blue eyes skidded to her brother. "I remember him. We crossed paths once or twice. You want me to use that to get to him?"

"Precisely. But only retrieve the loose diamonds and flush the small amount of drugs he carries," Jerry insisted. "I have no need for the rest of his cargo."

"That's it? Steal some diamonds and toss his drugs?" Cameron moved closer to see the assignment for himself.

"Well, no, that's the first step," Jerry said, pulling out a cigar and lighting it.

Narrowing his eyes, Cameron grabbed the file out of Bambi's manicured hands. "And how many steps are there?"

The mobster puffed on his Cuban and preened. "Just three. A measly three criminal acts, then you're free from all of us." He stepped closer and added, "But I think you'll get bored without all the action. A cop life only goes so far." He waved his cigar at Cameron. "You'll be back. Mark my words."

He shook his head. Keeping his temper reined in would take extra effort around these two. "Where's the intersect?"

"A gas station in Altoona. It's a big hub for human trafficking, and Mr. Wong is meeting with his business partner there. We'll be in touch with more details." Jerry smiled, then tucked Bambi's arm in his.

Cameron couldn't let that go. It was a line he couldn't ignore. If Donald Wong was smuggling humans, he'd make sure the police were informed right after his Del Rossi role was complete. He watched as the taillights of the black SUV melted away among the snowflakes. Then and only then did he exhale. Rubbing his hands together, he watched his cloudy puffs expand in the air.

The frigid temperatures were nothing compared to the struggle consuming his mind. He didn't have a choice, that much was abundantly clear. Jerry wouldn't hurt Joci, but Bambi was another story. She tended to color outside the lines—it was why they used to get along so well. He didn't want a mobster life anymore. Losing anyone out of his small group of loved ones would send him over the edge.

He turned on his toes. He couldn't live a life without Joci or his boys. He'd turn into everything the mob wanted from him if they weren't around. For tonight, he'd go home and hug Joci tight. He hadn't even started this last mafia job but realized it'd wear on their relationship. *We've been through worse.*

***

Joci unpacked the Chinese food recently delivered, then searched for a bottle of wine. "I know I bought one last week," she mumbled under her breath. The baby monitor whirred on the counter, but she didn't bother to glance over. They'd fall asleep soon. They just needed to chat first. It was cute how dependent they were on each other. Fraternal or not, they were twins.

"Aha! There you are." She grinned and opened the bottle of pinot gris and grabbed two glasses. Setting it all on the table, she nodded once. It didn't look like a romantic evening, with toys dotting the floor, but it was the best she could manage on short notice.

After the nanny left, Brett and Levi had seemed to know she had transcripts to review before dinnertime and subsequently demanded her attention. In the end, she'd shoved off work and spent time with her boys. Now that they were in their cribs, she turned her focus to her evening with Cameron.

"If he ever hurries up." She glanced to the clock on the microwave. He was an hour late. She looked at her phone, but no missed calls or text messages glared back. She bit her bottom lip, then remembered the plates. Normally, they didn't use them, but seeing how Rayna would be picking up the boys in the morning, Joci wanted to start off their weekend on the right foot.

Another ten minutes ticked by before lights shone through the front window. Joci stood and quickly fluffed her hair. Romance since Levi and Brett were born had been minimal. Even with all the help of friends and a nanny, they both fell into bed every night.

The front door opened, and she heard Cameron before she saw him. Taking a sip of wine, she nearly choked on it when he walked into the room. He was magnificent. His curly brown hair was plastered back, though from the looks of it, the gel was nearly gone. His police officer uniform stretched over his toned muscles, and the colorful tattoos on his wrists caught her eye. Underneath all those clothes lay the art she never knew she craved.

"Hey, beautiful," he greeted with a boyish grin. His brown eyes swept over the table. "Somebody's been busy."

She giggled and instantly swore under her breath at how giddy she must sound. Barely seeing him all week was torture. Before Cameron, she preferred sleeping alone. Hell, most of her life she preferred being alone. That all changed with him. The bed was lonely and missing something. Someone. If she never slept alone again, she'd be happy.

"Yeah, I thought I'd surprise you."

He pulled her in his arms and kissed her until she didn't remember the Chinese food slowly cooling nearby. "Any special reason?" he asked, moving back enough to nuzzle her nose and tuck her hair behind her ears.

"Other than hardly seeing you this week?" She threaded her fingers through his hair, releasing the curls. "It sucked, a lot."

"Believe me, I know." He lightly kissed her again. "You read my mind. I've been craving Chinese all day." He kissed her forehead. "I'm starving."

The moment he dropped his hold, Joci sighed. The man loved his food almost more than sleep. Smirking, she sat across from where he was already dishing out the various entrees and appetizers.

"How're the boys? Asleep?" he asked around a bite of sesame chicken.

"Yep." Joci scooped lo mein out of the white box and picked up her chopsticks. "You should've seen them earlier.

They're both as ornery as ever. Brett actually tossed his food at Levi tonight. It was so funny when Levi gave him the nastiest glare."

He nodded and shoveled fried rice in his mouth. "I bet that was adorable."

They ate in silence for a few minutes. Cameron glanced to her a few times but otherwise kept to the food. Sipping the egg drop soup, Joci frowned. Becoming parents had done a number on conversations too.

"Quinn said he'll stop by Rayna's tomorrow and help her out."

"Yeah, he told me." He didn't look up, seemingly distracted by whatever was on his phone.

Joci gritted her teeth. So far, nothing was piquing his interest.

"The next board meeting isn't for another month. I'm hoping by then I can convince them to let me out of Petosa Law." She watched him slurp a noodle.

"Cool. Good idea."

Digging out a crab rangoon, she tore it in half and dipped it in the sweet and sour sauce. "I'm thinking about cutting my hair really short and coloring it green."

"Mm-hmm, sure."

This time, she sighed loudly. Other than quickly glancing up, he didn't seem to understand her exasperation. Shrugging, he resumed picking through the white carton of orange chicken with his chopsticks.

Looks like it's time to drop the big bomb. She'd been

avoiding telling him until she could do it in person. This conversation wasn't appealing via text or even phone call.

"Adrian wants to go to counseling."

The chopsticks paused at his mouth, and his eyes met hers. "What?"

Joci held back an eye roll at the one subject that actually got his attention. "He thought it'd be good if I—we—talked to his therapist." She set down her spoon. "And he wants to talk to us about what happened when he was with the Mikkelsens."

Cameron let out a grunt, his top lip curling slightly. "And you think this is a good idea?"

"He's Brett's dad—"

"*I* am Brett's dad." His brows furrowed together, and a vein in his neck bulged.

Joci held up her hand. Evidently, she should've let him eat a little more before starting this conversation—even if it was the only one he engaged in. "Okay, you're right. Wrong choice of words there."

He scooted his chair backward and unlaced his boots. "Sorry I snapped. I don't like the idea of him and you…. Never mind." "Cam, you know I only care about him because he fathered Brett. That's it. If he disappeared again, I'd be totally fine with it."

"Yeah, I'm aware." He tossed the heavy boots to the corner of the room. "But with all that J.J. did or didn't do to Adrian, I don't think it's a good idea for you to be with him alone." He met her gaze. "Well, more than you already have to. I get that you work with him and have to for the time being, but I'd feel more comfortable if I went with you to the therapy session."

She took a sip of wine and nodded. "I agree. I didn't want it any other way. I was actually going to ask you to come with me."

"Okay, good. Glad we're on the same page." He returned to the food in silence, and Joci wanted to strangle him.

Pushing around the rice and orange chicken, she watched him eat. Suddenly, she wasn't hungry. Ten minutes passed, and she'd had enough. "Is anything wrong? You usually give a shit about us talking."

Cameron wiped his mouth with a napkin and tossed his phone to the table. His guarded brown eyes met hers, and hot tears crept to the surface. He reminded her of the mobster she met in the jail cell instead of the man she'd exonerated. Something had happened and he wouldn't tell her. It was more frustrating by the moment.

"I'm sorry. I hoped we could at least get through one day without bringing up our issues." He sighed and unbuttoned his shirt. "But we can't, because every time I meet your eyes, I feel guilty."

"What do you mean?"

"You should know before someone else tells you." He closed his eyes and rubbed his temples. "My ex-girlfriend is in town."

Joci didn't know how to react. While she was aware he had exes, he'd rarely spoken of any. The only one he'd mentioned was Jerry Del Rossi's sister. "Which one?"

"Bambina Del Rossi." He slowly opened his eyes and

their gazes locked. "She showed up the same day as Adrian. I didn't think it was the best timing to tell you with that surprise."

"Shit." She downed the rest of her wine and refilled the glass. "Is she why you didn't come home this week?" Horrible images ran through her mind of Cameron and his ex. While she didn't know what the girl looked like, Joci doubted the woman was ugly.

"Yes, but not because of whatever reason you're thinking."

She couldn't focus on anything but the pinot. "Is she staying for a while?"

"Unfortunately, yes. She's here for a job."

"Great." She stood and grabbed the bottle of wine before moving to the living room.

"Joce, hold up." Cameron followed, the chair scratching the floor with his quick movements. He made a frustrated sound when she didn't listen.

Plopping onto the love seat, Joci cradled the glass of wine and set the bottle on the side table. "I've been waiting, Cam. Waiting for you to come home. Waiting for us to talk and figure out how to be a couple with two infants. Now, I find out you've been staying away because your ex is in town. It doesn't take a lawyer to put together the motive behind you being gone."

"Dammit, Joci." He sat beside her and stole her wine. Setting it on the coffee table, he cupped her jaw in his hands. "You are the reason I exist. Not being next to you all these nights has been the worst form of torture." He searched her eyes, the truth indisputable in his steady gaze. "The only—and I mean only—reason I didn't come home is because I was afraid to tell you about Bambi. She's a bitch who I thought was out of my life." His lips grazed hers. "I don't want her. You are the only person I ever want beside me." He gently kissed her bottom lip. "And that's never fucking changing."

She licked her lips. He wasn't the most eloquent man, but he loved her with his entire soul. "You sure? Because these last few months haven't exactly been full of hot and sweaty sex like they used to be. I'm a mom, and that means my attention isn't always on you."

Chuckling, he pressed his lips to hers. "Aw, babe, you're all I need. Hot and sweaty sex or not, I'm here for the long haul. I love that you're an amazing mom even after a long day at court." He pulled her on top of him and locked his arms around her waist. "And not to brag, but I'm pretty sexy when I do laundry. I think I'm picking up this dad thing."

"You are a great dad, Cam. I never doubted it." She giggled and swept his hair off his forehead. "And you're right, you are damn sexy folding my underwear."

He kissed her neck, hands disappearing beneath her shirt. "I'm glad you think so." With one smooth move, he unclasped her bra and grinned. "Counselor, I do believe you're losing articles of clothing."

Playing along, she sat up and unbuckled his belt. She couldn't deny how his body came alive with the promise of more. It was something she'd never get sick of. "Me? Nah, I think you're mistaken, officer. You, on the other hand, may need to watch yourself, or I'll book you for indecent exposure."

Cameron smirked and tugged her shirt and bra off, flinging both toward the television. His eyes hungrily took in her naked torso. "Now that is a crime I'm willing to do time for." He leaned up and licked her nipple. "So long as you're in jail with me, that is."

Gasping, she clasped her hands around his neck and arched toward him. "And what exactly would we do in that jail cell?"

He paused and met her gaze. His voice lowered and he placed purposeful kisses on her chest and neck. "Fuck until the walls fall down around us." He captured her lips. "Then do it all over again."

Shivers ran down Joci's spine. "Promise?"

A determined grin covered his face. "Cross my heart."

CHAPTER THREE

Tugging up the heavy comforter, Cameron cuddled closer to Joci's body. Despite the space heater in the corner, the wind whipping against the house made him shiver. He tucked Joci flush to him and sighed at how perfectly she fit. Her long legs intertwined between his, silk compared to his skin.

Rayna had picked up Brett and Levi two hours ago. Cameron wasted no time before shedding Joci of her sweatpants and long-sleeved shirt. He couldn't get enough of her. Thankfully, her response seemed to mirror his. They had the rest of the day alone, and he'd spend it between Joci's legs if she let him. Judging from the small circles she drew on his arm, he doubted that would happen. She'd want to talk eventually.

"Why'd you and Bambi break up?"

The warmth he'd begun to appreciate dissipated into an arctic chill. The subject had been bound to come up sooner or later. He'd hoped it wouldn't be directly after sex.

"We wanted different things," he said at last, kissing the

back of Joci's neck.

She turned over to her back, her hazel eyes searching his face. "I need a little more explanation than that." She quirked her brow. "After all, you know everything about my past love life."

He chuckled. "True. All right, well, Bambi kept me in the mob. I thought she was like me—forced into servitude—but she was playing me the whole time. I found out she was Jerry's sister, but by then it was too late, and we were a couple." He paused and looked toward the window. "We were partnered because we had a knack for heists. You can guess the rest. As it turned out, she was the reason J.J. came after us." He kissed her nose. "Why he came after you."

"And that was because…?"

"J.J. was one of our crew. There were a couple other guys, plus Bambi and me. We had a huge heist ready to go. We could've retired off that money on some tropical beach, but Bambi got herself into some trouble with a guy she swindled."

"And you chose to save her instead of completing the job," Joci finished for him. "She's the one J.J. talked about."

"Yeah. I never thought much about it. I felt bad J.J. and the other two were pinched, of course. Jerry sent Bambi and me to Europe after that. Things were all right until she started doing things that even the Del Rossi mob wouldn't condone. She pissed off a lot of people and killed even more."

Cameron stopped and gazed down at Joci. She looked

gorgeous with her black-framed glasses slightly crooked and her hair spilling out of the messy bun on top of her head. Imperfection on her would always be perfection.

"So I gave Bambi the choice to disappear for an extended vacation or tell her brothers what she'd been up to. I even stashed money away for her and got her a new identity." He shook his head at the idiocy.

"What'd she choose?"

"Both, somehow." He brushed back a wisp of hair. "She went to her brothers and blamed me for getting her involved in the bad shit. After that, she went on her little vacation, though I doubt she actually did any relaxing."

"And Del Rossi extended your time with the mob?"

A painful smile crossed his face. "Yep. Oh, and a beating that left me with a broken arm. From then forward, she was dead to me. Honestly, I wish she'd stayed that way." He gently kissed Joci when she frowned. "But it doesn't matter. You and the boys are my everything."

Cozying closer, she pressed her lips to his neck. "Will you see more of her?"

"Yeah, I kind of have to."

She nipped his collarbone, and chills ran down his back. "Why?"

He thought about telling her the truth. Joci wouldn't like it, and she'd be constantly worried knowing he was involved with drugs and jewels. He couldn't decide which was worse.

"Because she's sticking around for a job. Hopefully, it

won't last long," he finally settled on. It was a half-truth at best.

Joci's tongue darted out and traced his nipple. "Is she pretty?"

Before he could answer, her teeth grazed him. A single touch from her was all he needed. Gripping her bun, he tipped her head back until her eyes met his. "Is somebody jealous?"

She bit her bottom lip, unable to nod. "Maybe."

Keeping his hold, he pressed his lips against her neck, moving up until he reached her mouth. His gaze searched hazel eyes filled with a mixture of longing and uncertainty. Hovering over her full lips, he looked between her mouth and her eyes. Life before her wasn't living. It was merely existing. She was more than worth the wait. Their future was worth his painful past.

"No one can take me from you, Joci." His lips brushed hers. "I'm yours for as long as you want me. And I hope it's a very, very long time."

She swallowed, the act harder than usual due to his grip, but he wouldn't relent. She needed to understand how much she meant to him. It was soul-deep and an endless sensation that couldn't be explained. He'd gladly show her every day until she accepted it.

"I'll always want you," she managed. The dedication shone in her stunning eyes, and his pulse quickened. Their connection wasn't one to be trifled with. He'd known from the start, but now, he couldn't deny they were always meant to be together. Fate be damned, she was his.

Cameron released his hold in time for their lips to collide in a heated frenzy. Joci pushed him to the bed, her kisses frantic. The blankets fluttered off the bed, and he gripped her hips, settling her on his lap in the most intimate way.

"But I do like seeing you all riled up, Mrs. soon-to-be Shearer," he said, tracing her engagement ring. "It's sexy."

"You know I haven't decided anything about my last name." Joci paused the movement of her hips and cupped his jaw. "But I can tell you this. Nobody takes what's mine. Whether we share a last name or not, I'm always yours."

"Good." He caught her lips before she could say another syllable. He didn't need to hear her words when he could feel her meaning.

***

Joci scrolled through the web pages, searching for the Federal case that would help her finish the final brief in a conspiracy case with a deadline the next day. Three days had passed since she and Cameron spent the day alone together. There was still something he wasn't telling her. She felt it in her gut. One of these days, she'd get it out of him. For the time being, she tried to focus on her research.

Voices carried from outside her office at Petosa Law. She glanced up and saw two forms pass by toward the smaller offices. While she wasn't fond of having desks at both firms, she couldn't deny how convenient it was to stop by Petosa after court. Since she was part owner, she'd also snagged Rayna a key card and office in the behemoth firm.

Balancing both locations was more difficult by the day, even though after her maternity leave, her case load hadn't picked up enough to overwhelm her, and Petosa Law only assigned a few cases to her. Those select few were with Adrian. She stopped typing and looked to her left, where his office was located. Just one wall sat between them, but it felt like a whole building. He didn't try to be chummy like he used to. She wasn't sure if she should appreciate the professionalism or be wary of it. Adrian was always a teetering balance of the two.

"Hey, Joce, are you ready for depositions?" Adrian asked, sticking his head in.

Speak of the devil. She locked her computer and stood. "Yeah, just one sec." After grabbing her legal pad and file, she met him outside her office. "Ready."

Adrian looked up from his phone and offered her a polite smile. "Great. We're using the conference room on the tenth floor. The court reporter is set up, and our client is being transferred from the penthouse."

They walked to the elevator, and Joci couldn't ignore the hushed words being said as they passed. Their reflection in the metal door caught her eye. Her red button-up shirt matched Adrian's red tie. From there, the similarities ended since she wore a gray skirt and matching jacket and he sported a black suit. Still, from the outside looking in, she'd guess they accidentally on purpose coordinated their clothes.

Stepping into the elevator, Joci smiled at Rayna when she

came out of her office, apparently looking for her. Rayna's gray eyes narrowed when she saw Adrian, but the door slid shut before Joci could say a word. Out of everyone, Rayna was the leeriest of Adrian. The reason why wasn't lost to her. Anyone who associated with Adrian was uneasy about his pop-up appearances. Petosa's board had made it clear that he should keep a low profile for the time being. After the last year, it was a good idea for all of them.

The ride down the few floors was quieter than usual. Neither said a word, and the only sound was Adrian's thumbs on his phone keyboard. Deciding now was as good a time as any, she turned toward him. His short red hair had been sleeked back but looked more masculine than greasy. His jaw was freshly shaved, and his clothes still held the familiar mix of dry cleaner starch and his cologne. Her throat dried the longer she stared at him. *Words, Joci, say words.*

"You can come by tonight to see Brett if you want."

Adrian looked over and smiled. "I'd like that. What time?"

"Right after depositions is fine." She eyed the clock on her phone. "That way you can feed him too."

The door sprung open, but neither moved. "Thanks, Joci."

She studied him curiously. There was something about him that sent bad shivers down her spine, but bits and pieces of the old Adrian shone through the cracks. "Come on, the sooner we get done, the sooner you can see how much your son eats."

"Are my two attorneys shagging?" An English accent broke into their conversation, and they moved toward the conference room, their client in tow. "Because honestly, you'd make adorable babies."

Adrian shot Mr. Huntly a pointed glare, which shut the man up for the moment.

Joci hid her smirk. Their client was flirty in all the right ways, or so said the witnesses they'd deposed an hour later. By the time they finished, she had scribbled plenty of ideas to weaken the state's case. She'd send some research ideas to her Petosa Law paralegal, since the next day was carved out for the Alley and Dorous firm.

Checking her text messages, she noticed one from Rayna about getting drinks later in the week. Another one from Quinn, asking if she knew what Rayna was doing the upcoming weekend. She rolled her eyes, and the last text set her mood to dismal.

Cameron: Hey, babe, I have to run by the gym after work. Not sure when I'll be home. Love you.

The *gym* was what he called Del Rossi business. Her thumbs hovered over a response. The ones she formulated didn't appease her, so she stuffed the device in her purse. *One of these days, I should drop by and have a conversation with Jerry.*

Her gaze dipped to the engagement ring on her finger. She'd give up all her riches if it meant Del Rossi didn't hold a knife to Cameron's throat at any given time.

She scanned the conference room. The state's attorney was chatting with the cute court reporter as she put away her gear. Adrian spoke with their client in quiet tones, most likely about the information divulged during the last few hours. It wasn't bad, but it wasn't good either. Being charged with fixing a lottery was never fun to deal with, in her opinion.

"You ready to go?" Adrian asked, and Joci realized she'd been staring off into space.

"Just need to grab my coat and purse from upstairs." She headed toward the elevator and watched their client wave from inside with two sheriff's deputies at his sides.

"He's going to get in trouble with his antics," Adrian noted, suddenly beside her.

"It seems like a requirement for Petosa clients." She chuckled and looked in his direction.

"I guess you're right." He hit the Up button. "Troublemakers are job security."

They watched the light at the top of the elevator blink before the arrow pointed down again. "I have therapy on Friday," he said so quietly, she wasn't sure she heard him correctly. "I'd like you to come with me."

Joci's brows rose, and she refrained from immediately responding. They'd barely talked at the office over the last few weeks, and now he wanted to have a conversation with a therapist. Her stomach dipped to a nosedive.

"Why don't we see how tonight goes?" she suggested, stalling.

His blue eyes dimmed slightly. "Sure, you bet."

Thirty minutes later, Joci unlocked her front door. She and Adrian walked inside, and a smile instantly spread over her face at the two babies sprawled out on their playmats. She tossed her purse and folders to the table, then shed her shoes and coat.

"How're my big boys?" she asked, plopping down in between them. Both babies turned their heads at the sound of her voice. Brett let out a little laugh, and Levi reached for her dangling necklace. She took turns kissing them loudly until they both giggled.

"You're such a good mom," Adrian said from his spot on the edge of the love seat. "You always were."

Sitting up, Joci patted the floor. "Brett likes playing with this giraffe." She handed it to him when he sat next to her. "He mostly puts it in his mouth, but it's his favorite. He can't sleep without it."

An odd expression covered Adrian's face. He set down the stuffed animal and carefully picked up the wriggling baby. For a moment, Joci simply watched the interaction between the two. Brett was near identical to Adrian, though she was fairly certain the baby had her nose.

Brett reached for Adrian's tie, his tiny fingers gripping it firmly before he brought it closer to his mouth. Adrian adjusted the baby on his lap and didn't seem to mind when the silk tie inherited drool.

"He's perfect." He touched the baby's soft red hair. "And big. Damn, I missed a lot."

When Levi started fussing, Joci picked him up. Kissing his chubby neck, she inhaled the idyllic baby scent. The good one that made her insides jumble, not the sour milk and dirty diaper one.

"Plenty of time to make up for it," she replied, nudging him with her elbow. "I'll let you two get acquainted while I check on the nanny."

Standing, she hoisted Levi on her left hip and made her way to the kitchen. Seeing the sixty-year-old nanny unloading the dishwasher, she smiled. "How were the boys today, Rita?"

Rita paused with silverware in her hand. "Those boys are *anges*," she replied with a slight French accent.

Adrian's father, Brett, had found Rita and paid for a year's salary as his maternity present to her. The only reason she'd agreed was because Rita wasn't anything like the other nannies she'd interviewed. Plus, Brett had had very limited time with his grandson before he passed away. She wasn't sure what they'd do once Rita returned to France in a few short months.

Joci tickled Levi's foot, the smile on his face worth his squirming. "Good to hear. You don't need to finish. I'll do it."

Nodding, Rita wiped her hands on the dishcloth. "I'll see you in the morning."

Waving Levi's hand, she watched the nanny leave before turning toward the living room. She stopped at the edge of the kitchen and felt her heart lighten just a little at the scene. Adrian had shed his jacket and lay on the floor while he carefully lifted Brett up and down from his face. The baby squealed and shrieked gleefully, patting Adrian's face every time he came close enough. Given how easily they'd bonded, no one would know he hadn't been there the last few months. But she knew, and she wasn't ready to forget.

Levi grabbed a handful of her hair and yanked, jerking her attention back to the curly-haired boy in her arms. "Well, aren't you an attention hog?" She nuzzled his tiny nose. "Sounds like somebody else I know." She placed him in one of the high chairs and moved about the kitchen, preparing their food.

After making two bowls of baby cereal, she placed one on the empty high chair tray. "Adrian, he's probably getting hungry. I have his dinner in here; you can feed him."

Adrian appeared moments later with a pouty-lipped Brett. He nodded. "Yeah, he was getting fussy." After strapping the baby into the high chair and putting a bib on Brett, he sat across from his son and picked up the bowl. "He likes this stuff?" He sniffed it and grimaced.

Joci spooned a bite into Levi's mouth. "Loves it."

"All right, here goes."

She watched him fumble with the little spoon, but eventually Adrian got the hang of it. By the end, cereal coated Brett's face and dribbled down his chin, but the huge grin on his face was well worth the mess.

"Wow, I said feed it to him, not help him wear it," she

teased, removing the bib. She lifted Brett out and nodded toward the bathroom. "Hey, I'm going to wash him off. Will you watch Levi, please?"

Adrian looked toward the other baby, playing with a soft-cover book. "Sure."

Following a quick bath where she was certain she got more wet than the baby, Joci wrapped Brett in a towel and grabbed a fresh set of clothes before returning to the living room. She stopped behind the rocking chair pointed toward the bay window and felt her heart swell at the sight of Levi sitting on Adrian's lap as they read a book. Levi's hands grabbed the fluffy touch-and-feel designs while Adrian read aloud. *I never thought I'd see this.*

She quietly walked farther into the room to listen. Thankfully, Brett was gnawing on his giraffe, perfectly happy with his towel apparel.

"You're cute too, you know? I never thought I'd say that about Shearer's kid." Adrian gently brushed back Levi's curls. "I wanted to hate you because you surprised everyone. But I can't. You'll always be Brett's best friend and brother and a part of my life too."

Levi leaned forward, but Adrian caught him before the infant completely toppled out of his arms. "Gutsy and headstrong. A perfect combo of your parents." He held Levi up to face him. The baby reached out and grabbed Adrian's nose, causing them both to laugh. "All right, let's make a pact. You keep Brett out of trouble, and I'll see to it that your daddy stays out of it too, okay?"

Tears filled her eyes at the sweet sentiment. The tender moment was one she'd never forget. *Maybe Adrian really did change.*

"Hey, Joce, you home yet? I need to grab—" Cameron's words fell flat when he walked in the entryway far enough to see Adrian holding Levi. His brown gaze turned black. "What're you doing here?"

Joci stepped into view. "Hey, what's up? I didn't think you were coming home until later."

Cameron met her gaze, and his brows furrowed. "I wasn't, but I needed to pick up my gym bag."

"Oh, you actually meant the gym." Laying Brett on the floor, she made quick work of his diaper and clothes. "I washed your shorts yesterday. They're probably still in the dryer." Standing, she watched the awkward, silent exchange between the men.

Walking over to Adrian, Cameron gently pulled his son into his arms. "Hey, buddy, missed you." He kissed Levi's cheek, and the baby cooed.

"I came by to visit Brett," Adrian explained, standing. "I'll go."

Joci moved to stop him, but Cameron blocked her. "Good idea. Next time, I'll be here to make sure everything goes okay."

Adrian seemed to understand the underlying warning. "Sure, if you want to set up a schedule or something—"

"Adrian, I'll see you tomorrow at work," Joci interrupted before Cameron could butt in. From the expression on his face, he wanted to do more than that.

"Yeah, you bet." Adrian quickly gathered his jacket and shoes. "About Friday…."

"Cam and I will be there." She offered him a small smile. He hadn't returned her text message about it, but if it meant figuring out Adrian's missing months away, he'd eventually agree.

Adrian stooped down and placed a kiss on Brett's cheek before silently leaving. The chilly air from his departure settled over Joci, and she whirled toward Cameron.

"What the hell were you thinking?"

Cameron set down Levi next to his brother and patted both their backs. "Funny, that's what I was going to say." He crossed his arms over his broad chest. "I thought I was clear about Adrian. I don't want him near my son or my house."

Joci clenched her jaw and shook her head in exasperation. "And I thought I was clear, he has a son here too, Cam. We talked about letting Adrian see Brett—"

"Yeah, when I was around."

She took a deep breath and closed her eyes. When she opened them again, Joci realized her failure. Cameron's one request was to be around whenever Adrian was. Obviously, that wasn't possible, but she'd promised to ensure he was nearby whenever Adrian had visits. After the craziness of the last year, she really should've tried harder to ensure Cameron's presence. Neither of them trusted Adrian, and she'd fallen back into the pre-mafia routine.

"You're right. I didn't think it would be a big deal to

have him over for a little bit, but I was wrong." She shifted on her feet. "I'm sorry."

The frustration in Cameron's features slowly disappeared. His shoulders slacked, and he unzipped the police officer coat. "I'm sorry too. I overreacted. I never thought I'd walk into our home and see Adrian holding my baby like that." His eyes drifted to the twins. "They looked pretty comfortable together, and that hurt."

Looping her arms around his waist, Joci hugged him tight. Only after he returned the hug did she speak. "He's not all bad."

He snorted. "He's not all good either."

"Neither are you."

Cameron tilted her chin up. "No, I'm not, but I wouldn't do anything to hurt my family."

"I know." She kissed his jaw, stubbled with dark hair. "Are you still going to the gym? Or meet with Jerry or whatever?"

"Nah, I'll hit up the one at work in the morning with Quinn. Jerry can wait too." He moved out of her embrace, but she pulled him back by the belt.

"You're up for Friday, right? If not, I can cancel."

He kissed the top of her head. "I don't like it, but I already switched shifts, so I better be."

"You know you're incredible, right?" She tugged his shirt free from his pants. His eyes turned into pools of dark chocolate, and a grin covered his face.

"I have heard it a few times."

"Oh, really? From anybody I know?" she teased, sneaking her hands beneath his shirt. The solid muscle there did not disappoint. *Screw the gym; he doesn't need it.*

"Maybe, maybe not." He grabbed her fingers, stopping their descent to below his pants, and lifted them above her head with one hand. He clucked his tongue and carefully pressed her back to the wall. "So eager, counselor. The morning sex wasn't enough for you?"

"It's been nearly twelve hours. I think I'm due." Her giggle morphed into an airy moan when his mouth found her neck.

"Insatiable. I love it," he growled.

Brett's little cry filled the room, throwing cold water on their embrace. Joci peeked over and saw Levi simply staring at his brother while he bawled.

"Tell you what, you handle that meltdown, and I'll make dinner." He quirked a brow, so she added, "And give you extra special attention tonight after they go to bed."

He kissed her hard, his tongue probing and tangling with hers. "I can't argue with that. What're we having?"

She gave him a knowing glance. "Leftovers."

Cameron chuckled and dropped her wrists before kissing her again. "Deal. Though, I might add conditions to the last one."

Walking toward the kitchen, she glanced over her shoulder and blushed when she noticed he was watching her backside. "Yes, sir, officer."

CHAPTER FOUR

The switch was easy enough. Cameron waited until the Asian businessman left his hotel room in Altoona before using the swiped key card for entry. From there, finding the locked suitcase full of gems wasn't too difficult. He heard Bambi's laugh float down the hallway, making him cringe. Her part of the theft only included flirting and a little drinking. Overall, he got the raw end of the deal. His ass was on the line more than hers, anyways.

Using his lock picking set, he soon heard the click of the locking mechanism. He opened the suitcase, his eyes widening at the stash inside. Jerry wasn't kidding when he said the businessman was loaded. In perfectly sectioned squares, emeralds, diamonds, rubies, and sapphires sat comfortably on silk pillows.

"I could start a whole new life with these," he mumbled, fishing out the fake diamonds from his pocket. As tempting as it sounded, he'd constantly be looking over his shoulder. That was no life for a family.

After he swapped out the fakes for the real diamonds, he carefully closed the suitcase. No tripwire sounded an alarm, so he returned the case to its spot in the closet. He found a small package of a white substance—heroin, if he had to guess—and flushed it as directed.

He looked through the peephole, and once no bodies met his view, slipped out into the hall. The surveillance cameras at the end of each hallway caught his eye. He'd looped the camera feed for their heist. Checking the time, he guessed they had another ten minutes before he and Bambi would become visible to the security guards.

Moving through the hotel, he walked into the attached restaurant and saw his partner at the bar, sipping moscato. She was flirting up their mark, Mr. Wong, while he stole the goods. From the looks of it, the Asian businessman would be extremely disappointed when he found out he wouldn't score with the blonde.

After meeting Bambi's gaze, he quickly escaped into the bitter night. The getaway car wasn't anything lavish, but then again, they wanted incognito, not flashy. He climbed into the driver seat and started the car. Less than five minutes later, Bambi hopped in the other side. Her posh perfume attacked his nose, and he rolled down the window, desperate for fresh air despite the freezing temperature.

"Jesus, did you bathe in that shit?" He shifted into gear and peeled out of the parking lot.

Bambi pushed back her blonde hair and shot him a beguiling grin. "Aw, you're already thinking about me in the tub."

"Yeah, only to drown you," he mumbled.

Her laughter sounded like nails on a chalkboard. "Always a joker. No wonder Jerry likes you. He's too soft when it comes to funny guys." She buckled her seat belt. "Let me see the diamonds." When he didn't respond, she reached over and dug through his pocket.

"Dammit, stop. I'll get them." He pushed away her hands, and she clapped giddily. "Fuck, you're annoying."

"Yeah, yeah, show me the jewels."

Cameron tossed the black velvet bag to her. "Who's fencing them?"

Bambi sprinkled some of the diamonds in her palm. "You."

He swung his gaze to her and shook his head. "What? I can't do that. Hell, no."

She carefully put the gems away and tucked the bag in her cleavage. "Why not? You always did when we worked together."

He turned the corner a little too sharply, and she bumped her head on the window. "And I haven't done a heist in nearly a decade. My contacts are probably all dead."

She shrugged. "Find new ones. You're a cop, shake down some criminals."

Cameron gripped the steering wheel until his fingers hurt. They traveled in silence, the rock and roll radio station the only sound beyond the whistling wind around the car.

"Why'd you come back, Bambi? You could've lived

comfortably anywhere. I put plenty of money in that account." He glanced over and saw her picking at her cuticles.

"I got bored, Cameroni. The men were all the same. The heists too easy." She batted her long lashes at him. "You're the only person I had fun with."

"Too bad. That's never happening again." He focused on the road, careful not to hit the black ice.

"I didn't think so either when I saw you with her. Joci. That's her name, right?" He glared at her, but she just laughed. "The two of you are sweet. She's all venom and sass, and you're the antidote. You have some adorable kiddos too. That little Levi—"

He slammed on the brakes. "Shut up, Bambi. Don't talk about my family."

"Calm down, big daddy." She scoffed. "I don't care about them or you anymore. I wanted to ruffle your feathers." She looked him up and down. "Looks like I did a good job too."

He pushed on the gas again and thanked his stars when the rendezvous spot came up on the right. They'd go their separate ways, and he was more than ready. Hitting up the gym sounded too good to pass up. He needed to punch something.

Bambi hopped out first when they stopped. "Don't forget, we need a fence for the diamonds. Jerry wants it done by next Saturday." She patted the hood of the car. "Get to it."

He clenched his hands into fists, willing himself to calm down. He couldn't. Not with the black SUV nearby, undoubtedly with Jerry Del Rossi waiting inside. Bambi waved, then climbed into the car. The driver revved the engine and screeched out of the empty lot.

Letting out his breath, Cameron swore loudly. He walked over to his Jeep and unlocked it. When he closed the door, he slapped the steering wheel. He didn't know how much longer he could endure being at Bambi's beck and call. She'd kill him without a second thought, and he couldn't afford that. He had too much to live for now.

***

The notifications on Joci's computer glared angrily at her. While she spent two days at Petosa and three at her own firm, there didn't seem to be enough hours in the day to get everything done. She printed the last set of police reports and rolled her neck from side to side. To her dismay, it didn't help loosen the kink.

"Rayna, how do you feel about hiring a law clerk for a while?" she called after realizing the coffee in her cup was no longer warm. She walked to the small kitchen area and filled the coffeepot with water.

Heeled shoes clicked on the floor and then Rayna Alley stood in the entryway. She leaned against the refrigerator and crossed her arms over her lavender shirt. "I'm okay with that. I can probably find someone at Drake University. Maybe a second- or third-year law student?"

Joci opened the coffee tin and inhaled the heady scent. It was one of her favorites. She scooped the grounds into the filter and pressed the button to brew. "Sounds good to me."

"Is this request because of Petosa or because you think we actually need one?"

"Both." She watched the coffee slowly trickle into the glass pot. "I feel overwhelmed with everything lately."

Rayna snorted. "Yeah, probably because Adrian is around again and you're forced to work with him." She shivered. "Is it just me, or is he creepy?"

Chuckling, Joci shrugged. "In a way, he is. I'm going to his therapy session after work today."

"Excuse me, what?"

"With Cam," she added before the redhead across from her came unglued. Though Rayna was never in any danger with the Mikkelsen mob, she was around to see the ramifications in her best friend's life.

"Good. You need somebody with you. I don't trust Adrian." She grabbed a mug from the cabinet above the sink. "Which reminds me, I never asked how you were doing after Adrian's triumphant return. Everyone focused on Adrian, and I get it, but I didn't check on you. I'm sorry."

She brushed her fingers through her hair. "It's fine, Ray. He hasn't been back that long."

"Long enough to cause a rift between you and Cameron," Rayna pointed out.

She didn't want to admit her friend was right, but she wasn't far off. "It's been weird. I'll look over at Adrian and totally forget what he did. Other times, our eyes connect and I want to throttle him for putting us all in danger."

Rayna grabbed the now full coffeepot and poured fresh cups for them. "Are you having second thoughts about him?"

"No. That'll never happen."

"You also said that about getting involved with a client," Rayna said over the top of her mug.

"I think Cam and I qualify for the exception." Joci blew on the steaming liquid. "Brett needs his dad. I'll encourage Adrian's involvement, but I'm not holding my breath that he changed. Underneath the scars, he's the same attorney who gambled with his life and ours."

"Well, I'm glad to hear it." Rayna sipped the coffee. "Now, on to a better topic, have you seen the new attorney at Petosa? Holy hell, he is fine." She fanned herself dramatically. "Those blue eyes are to die for."

Rolling her eyes, Joci was grateful for a business partner who could go from man bashing to man crushing in the same conversation.

***

Five o'clock came sooner than Joci anticipated. The trip to the law library helped burn most of her afternoon, and when she received the reminder text message from Adrian, she finished up her research and headed toward the therapist's office.

She rubbed her lips together anxiously until she saw Cameron's Jeep pull into the parking lot. Going to therapy was one thing, but going with Adrian was a whole other event. She was never more grateful for the man heading her direction. Getting out of her Mercedes, she waited until Cameron caught up with her.

"Hey," she greeted, hugging him tighter than normal. His masculine scent comforted her the longer she stayed in his embrace. If she could remain there all evening, she would.

He kissed the top of her head. "Hey, yourself. You all right?"

"I am now." She patted his chest and smiled when her fingers grazed the police badge. He was the real deal. No matter what anyone said, she couldn't deny that people could change if they truly wanted. He was case in point.

Then maybe Adrian can change too. She shook the thought away for the time being. On the surface, Adrian appeared to be different, but she couldn't make any determination quite yet.

Pulling back, she smiled. Cameron was delectable. No matter the time, he looked ready to rumble. He sported a new bruise under his right eye, and she guessed it had to do with catching a criminal during his shift. *Oh, how the tides have turned.*

"You sure about therapy? Because I'm perfectly okay with turning around and going to Fong's for some pizza." He jerked a thumb over his shoulder, his face hopeful.

Looping her arm around his waist, she shook her head. "Sorry, we need to do this. But afterward, I'm game for Fong's. Maybe I can convince Rayna and Quinn to meet us there."

"Believe me, Quinn will make it if Rayna's there."

"Is he still afraid to ask her out?"

Cameron chuckled. "Something like that."

They walked up the sidewalk and into the high-class office building. There were several other business suites, but they wanted the man on the fifth floor. To her relief, no one else got on the elevator with them. The metal box slowly ascended, and so did Joci's anxiety.

"Hey, it's gonna be okay." He squeezed her hand. "And if not, I'll be here for you. I make a great getaway driver."

"Thanks, Cam. That means a lot." She kissed his cheek just as the elevator doors slid open. Adrian stood on the other side, and his face momentarily dipped into a frown when he saw them.

"You're here, good," he said, walking the other direction. "I wasn't sure if you bailed."

"Nope, we don't do that shit, unlike some people," Cameron loudly replied.

Joci's eyes bulged in warning, but he merely shrugged. She walked into the lobby, and her stomach dropped. It hadn't changed much since she was there last. A saltwater aquarium sat on the east wall, and the chairs were organized in a wide square.

After Adrian checked them in, they sat on opposite sides, silence ensuing. Joci picked up one of the magazines from the seat beside her, pleasantly surprised it was that month's edition instead of being years old.

"Thanks again for coming," Adrian finally said.

Joci glanced over to him and noticed he was bouncing

his leg. His hair was slightly ruffled, as if he'd ran his hands through it nervously. "We're here for Brett."

She opened the magazine and heard Adrian sigh. She couldn't give him hope for anything other than a business relationship. He didn't deserve one after the last year.

"Sure, yeah."

She peeked up when Cameron stood and walked over to the fish tank. He bent over and studied the brightly colored fish. Looking over at Adrian, she caught him staring at her. Awkward was putting it lightly. Clearing her throat, she returned her gaze to the magazine article. Thankfully, they didn't have to endure the silence long.

"All right, Mr. Petosa, I'm ready for you." The therapist, a man in his sixties, stopped at the edge of the waiting room and smiled. "Joci, so glad to see you again." He looked to Cameron. "And you must be Joci's fiancé. I'm Dr. Randall." He waved. "Come on back, kids. Let's chat."

"Last chance to escape," Cameron whispered as they followed Adrian and the doctor to the office down the hall.

She playfully poked his side. "I wish."

"Have a seat anywhere. There's plenty of room," Dr. Randall said with a smile once Cameron entered last. After closing the door, he returned to the white chair between the two couches.

Joci and Cameron sat on one couch, while Adrian took the other to himself. She squeezed Cameron's knee once. His strength would be needed no matter how the next hour went.

"Okay, so Adrian asked you to come because we've been working on his mental health over these last months," Dr. Randall began. "You're both crucial to his betterment and will be involved throughout his life. I want to give Adrian a chance to explain himself in a safe, controlled location." He nodded to his client. "Whenever you're ready."

For a minute, no one spoke, the fan oscillating above them the sole sound in the room. She exchanged a worried glance with Cameron. He seemed more uncomfortable than her with the whole situation. If the roles were reversed, she would be too.

"J.J. and I were in the car beside the one that blew up. The blowback from the explosion hit us and resulted in excruciating injuries." Adrian kept his eyes fixed on the glass table between the two couches. "I didn't really know what happened until I woke up the next day. In Mexico, of all places. I remember J.J. being pissed because things didn't go down like he wanted. He was adamant that he'd make Cameron pay."

Dr. Randall quietly jotted down notes from his seat, and Joci's palms felt slick. She didn't want to imagine all that had happened to Adrian, but she was anyways. She'd agreed to this meeting, after all. Walking away wasn't an option. She needed to hear just as badly as he needed to share.

"I heard him talk to the surgeon before they put me under. He asked him how to permanently delete someone from memories. That guy couldn't do it, but he did manage to bandage me up." Adrian rolled up his sleeves and surveyed the scarred flesh there. Joci winced at the sight, and Cameron squeezed her shoulder. "Not the best, but it's only skin deep."

"Okay, I'm going to jump in really quick, Adrian," Dr. Randall said. "If you can, tell Joci and Cameron what else J.J. did to you personally. It may help them understand."

Adrian looked to Cameron but didn't make full eye contact. When his eyes moved to her, Joci recognized the pain in his blue depths. It sent a shiver down her spine. Suddenly, she knew what he'd say would be difficult to hear.

"He fucked with my brain." Adrian let out a breath and stared at the floor. "He found some psycho scientist and he did shock therapy on me." He met her gaze again and laced his hands together. "It was mostly about you, Joce. He tried to turn any good feelings I had for you into bad ones." A sad smile crossed his face. "But they couldn't." He swallowed hard. "So they changed it to Cameron after a month."

Tears filled Joci's eyes at the thought. She'd never been even remotely close to tortured, but it sounded horrible. Cameron's arm rested at the back of the couch, and he moved a little closer to her, almost as if he was trying to protect her from the words.

"Not surprisingly, I had physical ailments that kept me all but chained to the bed. J.J. would only let me do physical therapy if I passed his tests. They started out okay, but I didn't realize what he was doing until later."

Cameron laced his fingers with hers, and she squeezed them, thankful for his presence.

Adrian rubbed his lips together. "I tried to fight it." He met Joci's gaze, and she saw the unshed tears. "I really did, but after a while, I gave in and let the hatred flow through me. It made the pain go away and that's all I wanted. J.J. stopped once I was pissed enough. I thought I could just forget it all once I was home again."

Joci brushed away the tears steadily streaming down her cheeks.

"One afternoon, I woke up and couldn't remember what I'd done that morning. It freaked me the hell out." He looked to Dr. Randall. "I now know they tweaked my brain just enough to do whatever they wanted me to. It got so bad I thought I had amnesia that came and went with each day. After I got back to Des Moines, the neurologist said it was one of the best and worst things she'd seen with memory manipulation."

"Wait, so you acted like a douche because some crazy doctor gave you amnesia?" Cameron piped up to ask. He moved to the front of the couch cushion and tented his hands.

Adrian nodded. "In a way, yes. J.J. brainwashed me until I thought everything I did was to help Joci get rid of you, Cam." He frowned the moment the words were aired. "Sorry about that."

Dr. Randall flipped to a new page, and Joci wondered what the hell the man could be writing about. It wasn't new information, but maybe their presence made a difference in Adrian. The attorney side of her wanted to see those notes.

"What about the mind bombs J.J. said he put in you?" Cameron narrowed his gaze first on Adrian, then the therapist. "He said he installed trigger words to make you do things even after he was gone."

Adrian looked to Dr. Randall. "I honestly don't know. It's a possibility."

"Adrian and I are working through normal words and phrases to see if he has any adverse reaction to them," Dr. Randall informed them, crossed his left leg over his right. "So far, nothing."

"Then there's a possibility J.J. wasn't lying about that?" Joci asked, adjusting her glasses.

"Unfortunately, yes. The brain is a very complex organism, and science hasn't mapped out everything it can do." Dr. Randall's brown eyes seemed disappointed by his own statement.

"All right, so fast forward, you're physically better because you mentally shut down. Now, months later, you're mentally stable, and your next act is to do what? Win Joci back and hope for the best?" Cameron stood and paced.

Adrian grimaced. "I want to get to know my son and be in his life." He met Joci's eyes. "While there's nothing more I'd like than to be a family with Joci and Brett alone, I understand she loves someone else. I'm working on accepting that."

"But you haven't, have you?" Joci chimed in.

He shook his head. "No, I haven't. It may take longer than either of you want, but I truly am sorry for what I did when I was under J.J.'s manipulation. I won't make excuses, because I fucked up. I wasn't in control of everything, but I accept responsibility for the pain I've caused. I'm asking you to give me a second—or third in your case, Joce—chance."

Cameron perched his hands on his hips. From the corner of her eye, Joci sensed Adrian's gaze on her, but she couldn't reciprocate. There was too much funneling through her mind at the moment.

"Joci, you've only engaged a small amount in this appointment," Dr. Randall stated. "Can you tell me your thoughts on this?"

She tucked her straight hair behind her ears and met the therapist's friendly gaze. "My thoughts? I have many, but I need to go through them myself. I like seeing the facts and evidence, going over them hundreds of times, analyzing the case before I can completely understand." She wiped her palms on her thighs. "I think I need to see the research behind mind control or brainwashing and as much as I can about things related to the brain before I can make any kind of decision about Adrian."

Dr. Randall smiled and nodded appreciatively. "I have to commend you, Joci. You've come a long way since we used to meet." He looked to Cameron. "I'm glad your personal growth has extended to the people you surround yourself with. Healing takes as long as you need it." He scribbled something down. "Don't you agree, Adrian?"

"Yeah, of course. Whatever you need, Joce." Adrian forced a smile. It clearly wasn't the outcome he wanted, but it was all she could offer at the moment.

Dr. Randall switched gears slightly to lighten the mood. After each person offered a brief explanation of their relationships and jobs, Joci felt her stomach ease slightly.

She could talk about the law and her twin boys all day long. When it came to Adrian, she'd rather clam up than explore.

Cameron seemed to take to the doctor when the two started discussing their favorite rock bands. Whenever the conversation turned toward Adrian, though, Cam's edge reappeared. He was just as uncomfortable with the man as she was. They were on the same page in that regard.

"All right, kids, our time is up." Dr. Randall stood. "If you're interested, we can meet again next week."

Getting to her feet, Joci shook the doctor's hand and retreated to where Cameron stood by the door. "We'll think about it. Thanks."

Cameron led them out of the office before Adrian could get a word in. She didn't want to talk out her feelings just then. She needed to drink them. *And do research. Lots and lots of research.*

CHAPTER FIVE

From his spot on the floor with the boys, Cameron watched Joci talk on her cell phone. A week had come and gone since their visit to Adrian's therapist's office. They seldom spoke about it, and Joci had spent the last week avoiding Petosa Law Firm. He couldn't blame her, but he was worried. She'd taken on five intense cases in the last three days alone. Normally, he wouldn't be concerned, but when she started forgetting things like Levi's favorite blanket at bedtime and the doctor appointment for the boys, Cameron couldn't ignore it any longer.

He tickled Brett's little toes and blew a raspberry on his belly. Times like these were ones he treasured more than any other. Being a dad hadn't been in the cards for him. At least, he didn't think so as of two years ago. These days, he wouldn't trade it for a world free of mobsters.

Joci paced from the kitchen to the bedroom hallway. She was helping Rayna prep for her trial the next day. From where he sat, she was working on flattening the new carpet more. Adrian was on her mind, and it bugged the hell out of him. He took the empty bottles away from the twins and set them on the side table. He'd get to the dishes later. Right now, he was spending time with his boys.

The clock struck nine, and Cameron carefully grabbed both boys in his arms. He paused in the hallway long enough for Joci to give Levi and Brett kisses. She smiled fleetingly at him before returning to her conversation.

"All right, boys, it's jammie time." He placed Levi in his crib and Brett on the changing table. "Let's see, how about these cute little bears?"

He held up the onesie sleeper sporting cartoon bears with tiny stocking caps. Brett scrunched up his nose, and Cameron caught his breath. In that moment, the baby took on Joci's trait. "Holy shit. Just when I thought I couldn't love you more."

Brett giggled and batted at the pajamas, so Cameron dug out a camouflage onesie, which won for the night. After finishing up with the redheaded cutie, he zoomed Levi to the table and held up two options. Levi's chubby hands instantly picked out the dinosaur set.

"My kind of pj's," Cameron said, snuggling his nose to his son's neck.

Tucking both boys all outfitted for bed in the crook of his arms, Cameron sat in the rocking chair next to their cribs. He picked up one of the books with fuzzy farm animals and started reading. Levi immediately patted the furry creatures on each page, while Brett sat back and simply sucked his pacifier and cuddled against Cameron's chest.

By the time he finished the book, the twins were halfway to dreamland. Cameron gently laid Brett in his crib, making sure his giraffe was nearby. Levi's bottom lip quivered ever so slightly when Cameron settled him in the crib. He touched one of Levi's curls, the corkscrew too adorable for him to fathom how it came to be in his life.

"I'm one lucky son of a bitch," he whispered, tracing Levi's cheek with his knuckles. He double-checked Brett before sneaking toward the exit. He let out a sigh of relief when he closed the door behind him and neither cried.

Returning to the living room, he began picking up the discarded baby toys, bottles, and pacifiers. Normally, he wasn't around to put them to bed. Sensing that Joci needed him at home instead, he'd switched shifts today. *Good thing I did. Doesn't look like the cleaning service has come yet this week.*

He plopped the dirty dishes in the sink and filled it with suds. Right before he dug into the chore, his phone rang from the ledge above the sink. He wiped his hands on the back of his sweatpants and frowned at the blocked caller ID.

"Hello?"

"Aw, Shearer, those little *bambinos* are stupidly cute." Bambi's voice skittered across the line.

He ground his teeth together. "What do you want?"

"Jerry says you haven't fenced the diamonds yet. What's the holdup?"

"My criminal informant flaked on me." He pulled the

curtain over the kitchen window. "I need more time."

"Sorry, the mob doesn't work that way. You should know this by now." She sighed, the act supposed to be sad but sounding the complete opposite. If he knew her—and he did—she was filing her nails as they spoke. *Probably into points to stab me.*

"It's not like I can go out in the open with this. I'm a cop. I have to be careful or I'll lose my job." Cameron closed his eyes and shook his head. "But that's probably what Del Rossi wants, isn't it?"

"It wouldn't be so bad, now would it? Endless jobs, swimming in money, and—"

"And living on the bad side of the law. No, thank you. I'm a shady dude, I won't deny that, but I'm on another path now. Once this job is over, I won't think twice about leaving the mafia."

Bambi chuckled, then rattled off something in Italian to someone on her side. "Ticktock, Shearer. You have until tomorrow night, or Jerry promised I could punish you for disappointing him."

He didn't have to hear the click in his ear to know she'd hung up. Scrolling through his contacts, his thumb hovered over one name he'd hoped to never use again. "Fuck." He hit Send and waited for the call to connect. This last job was making him return to his Ohio roots. That thought scared him more than the mafia boss on the other side of town.

***

"Joce, I'm heading out. Be back later," Cameron called. Before Joci could wipe the spit-up from her sweatshirt, the front door latched shut.

"Hmm, guess it's just you cuties and Mommy for a while." She bopped Levi's nose with her finger. "Who wants to go ice skating?"

The twins gave her blank stares.

"Yeah, you're right, you guys aren't ready for skating," she teased, tickling Brett's side. The baby giggled and cooed, reaching for her. "How about the grocery store? Think we can handle that?"

Not waiting for their response this time, she placed them on the play mat. She surveyed the damage from their breakfast and pouted. "Okay, boys, hang tight. I'll finish this up, then we'll go." She glanced over and smirked when she saw them perfectly happy simply staring at themselves in the tiny mirrors.

An hour later, Joci struggled with the two car seats. She snagged a cart and put Brett in the top section, then settled Levi in the buggy part.

"They really should come up with some sort of contraption for moms of twins so they can go to the grocery," she grumbled, entering the local store. She unzipped their coats, since both tended to overheat. "Let's see, what do we need?" Fishing through her pockets, she held up the crinkled list. "We're just going to ignore the spit-up on here, aren't we?" She glanced between Levi and Brett. Both wore mischievous grins.

She guided the cart down the aisles, setting the food around Levi's car seat. By the time she finished, she swore she'd start paying someone else to go to the store for her. *It'll only get worse as they age*, she figured, unloading the food onto the conveyer belt at the checkout.

Joci took a deep breath of winter air when she finished twenty minutes later. She gripped the cart handle and looked at Levi. The little bugger had decided it was a fabulous time for a blowout right when she was halfway done with the cashier. Thankfully, the store hadn't been too busy, but she'd had to put her groceries on hold while she took the duo to the bathroom.

She clicked the car seats in place before she loaded the groceries into the trunk. At the last bag, two loud voices drifted through the parking lot. Curious at the commotion, she peeked her head around the Mercedes and spotted two men near the west side of the grocery store. At a glance, she'd guess they weren't merely sharing a smoke. Her eyes widened when she recognized the taller of the two men.

"What the hell?" She closed the trunk and turned on the automatic car starter. Walking to the front of the car, she squinted. Sure enough, her loving fiancé stood with a cigarette between his lips and a wool cap pulled low to his eyes.

"What is he doing here?" She couldn't fault him for going to the grocery store, but he wasn't inside. He was acting sketchy in the alley beside the store.

She checked on the twins and found them chewing toys,

so she kept watching Cameron and his shady friend. Their voices lowered, and Cameron handed the guy something discreetly. It looked like a brown paper bag. Money, if she had to guess, but she was too far away to be sure. Her mind spun with different explanations. There were plenty of legal ones, but she could only focus on the illegal ones. *Why else would he be sneaking around?* She bit her bottom lip and climbed into the driver seat.

Dialing Cameron's number, she waited as the call rang through the car's audio system.

"What's up?"

"Hey, so the boys and I are running errands and thought we'd meet you for lunch." She watched him closely. He'd finished his transaction and walked toward his Jeep parked on the far end of the neighboring parking lot. "Where are you?"

Wind whipped around him and garbled his voice. "Just heading to the station. I had some reports to finish," he replied, and Joci's stomach dropped.

"Oh, okay. Well, if you're busy, we can do something for dinner." She gripped the steering wheel and watched his Jeep disappear in the direction opposite of the police station.

"Sounds good, babe. Gotta go."

Music replaced Cameron's voice, the children's songs no longer cheerful in her mind. "He lied. That asshole lied." She shifted into Reverse. "But why?" No answer came to her, disturbing her further. "I thought we were past the deceit. He told me stuff even when it was about the mob."

She scrunched her nose and drove toward home. Once the boys were down for their naps, she'd do some investigating of her own. Cameron wasn't as good a mobster as he thought. He always left a trail, and she was determined to follow it.

***

Easing the Jeep into the drop-off location at Grey's Lake, Cameron turned down the rock radio station. Days like this one, he could go for a few hours on a drum set to steady his nerves. He scanned the area and saw no one else braved the cool temperatures. It wouldn't stay like that for long. Spring was nearly upon them, and it was equally as fickle as the remaining seasons in Iowa. The snow on the ground could melt within the week for all he knew.

Another car drove up the rocky drive, and the headlights flashed at him. *That must be the guy.* He checked his handgun and placed it in the small of his back. His Ohio gang contact had been leery to give him the fence in Iowa, but eventually Cameron won out. It took more money than he expected, but that was Trey. The guy would fold once enough zeroes were at the end of a number.

Now, he sat across from a stranger who probably had a warrant or two out for his arrest. The cop side of Cameron warred with the mobster side. *One last job.*

He got out of the Jeep and pulled up his hood. Being photographed by anyone wasn't happening today or any other day. He'd learned from J.J. that the best way to hide was in plain view.

"You Shearer?" the other man asked, his long beard fluttering in the breeze.

"Last I checked." Cameron stuffed his hands in the pockets of his jeans. "Trey said you'd know my fence."

"Yeah, I can set up a meet for next week."

Cameron's stomach churned. Jerry had demanded the exchange by the following day. Pressing the envelope with his mob boss didn't sound like a good plan, but he didn't have any other choice. If he pushed Trey's contact, the man may scurry to some hole and never resurface. It took one bribe to Trey, one bribe to Trey's number-two man, and now this jerk would be another load of money for the sake of Del Rossi. Money talked in the mobs, and Jerry Del Rossi didn't mind dishing it out to get his way.

"All right, sure. You have my number."

The man nodded and held out his hand. "The money?"

Cameron pulled out the envelope and offered it to him. "Half today, half when it's done."

"That's not what—"

"Well, that's how I do business," he interrupted, lifting the cash before the other man could snatch it. "I was promised an immediate deal. Since you're making me wait, I'll do the same for you."

"Fine." His contact snorted and grabbed the offered money before retreating to his vehicle.

Not waiting around for someone to see him, Cameron trudged back to his Jeep and started it. His phone lit up with a new message. Checking it, he groaned at the picture from

Joci. It was of Brett and Levi sporting baby Nike shoes. He'd bought them not long after they were born, and until now, they didn't fit.

He sent a reply and put the car into gear. Lying to Joci earlier didn't feel good. He hated every word of the lie meant to protect her. Any other time, he would've fessed up, but this time around was different. The players weren't ones he knew. At least not anymore. Joci would figure it out; she was smart like that. He just hoped he could tell her the truth before she assumed the worst.

CHAPTER SIX

The courtroom was extra packed on Friday when Joci took her seat beside Adrian. No doubt the gallery was full due to their client fighting the vehicular manslaughter charge. The day before hadn't been as bad, but today, two news reporters had come to hear the closing arguments.

She watched the jury fill in the empty seats and sat once the judge loudly banged his gavel. Her portion of the trial had wrapped up yesterday with the witnesses. Since the case began when she was on maternity leave, her role was secondary. Cross-examination of the state's witnesses was all she was tasked with, and that was plenty for the quick turnaround.

Their client, a young kid who fell asleep at the wheel and crashed into another car, tapped his finger against his other arm nervously. The whole trial had been one mass of anxiety for the man, who potentially faced the better portion of his life behind prison bars.

Focusing back on Adrian, she had to admit his closing

statement was bulletproof, touching the emotional side of the jury more so than the state's. It wasn't a case she liked, but attorneys didn't always get to be picky with who paid their retainers.

"My client made a mistake. He got behind the wheel after studying for his midterm exams. If you ask him now, he'd say it was the worst thing he could've done." Adrian paused and slowly reviewed the jury. "No one could've predicted what happened. I'm sure many of you have driven after a long day and fallen asleep behind the wheel too. We can't destroy this young man's future, because that's what you would be doing if you find him guilty."

Joci closely watched the jury. While she couldn't tell which direction they leaned, she was well aware of the spell Adrian created with words. The dark blue shirt beneath his black suit didn't hurt matters either since both accentuated his eyes.

His charisma was only part of the reason why the jury couldn't keep their eyes off him. In passing, she'd overheard two of the jurors discussing how good-looking Adrian was with the mysterious scar on his cheek. Joci had to admit, it gave him the bad-boy vibe, and he no doubt had no issues getting a date. *Ew, why are you thinking about that?* She shook her head, hoping to stop herself of going down that path even more.

"You must acquit Mr. Harpin or justice will never be served." Adrian nodded once, then turned toward his seat. He offered her a small smile and closed the distance, his limp evident until he reached the table. Normally, she didn't notice it, but his leg seemed to be paining him more today. A sheen of sweat lined his brow, and she hoped he hadn't overexerted himself. While she didn't know the full extent of his injuries, she doubted an intense trial was helping his recovery.

The judge dismissed the jury to their negotiations and disappeared to chambers. The courtroom immediately echoed with new conversations.

"You did great," she praised.

"Thanks." He started gathering his files into an orderly pile. "You did too."

Joci nodded, but before she could respond, Adrian swayed to the right and gripped the side of the table. "Are you okay?" she asked, taking in his white face.

He met her gaze and opened his mouth to speak, but suddenly crumpled to the floor, clutching his chest.

"Oh my God, Adrian!" She quickly moved to help him, as did the two deputies nearby. Checking his wrist, she was momentarily relieved to feel the strong pulse.

"What happened?" one of the deputies asked, examining Adrian's limp body. The other deputy called for an ambulance.

By now, a crowd had gathered around them. Joci swallowed hard and tried to calm her fear. "I don't know. One minute he was talking, and the next, he fainted."

"All right, hold tight. The paramedics are on their way," the second deputy informed. He addressed the crowd.

"Give him some room. EMTs will be here shortly. I'm sure he'll be fine."

Joci wasn't as confident as the deputy. She stayed by Adrian's side until two paramedics showed up and wheeled him out of the courthouse on a stretcher. She couldn't remember any of her responses and barely noticed the late spring snowstorm outside.

"You the wife?" a pretty blonde asked when they reached the ambulance. Joci recognized the driver as Tad O'Brien, the paramedic who somehow seemed to get any case involving her group of friends.

The wind whipped at Joci, her fingers still gripping the side of the stretcher. "Um, yes, I mean, no. Well, I was." She adjusted her glasses. "He's my son's dad."

The woman lifted her brows. "All right, then. Hop in. You can fill us in on any medical history you know."

"Okay." Joci climbed into the back of the ambulance. She gave the paramedics a basic rundown of Adrian's health. The last few years were blank, and those were the most crucial ones. After a short ride, the ambulance arrived at Mercy Hospital. When they reached the ER doors, Adrian's heart monitor beeped loudly.

"He's flatlining," the blonde said, hopping on top of the gurney to perform chest compressions while Tad pushed through the doors.

"What's happening?" Joci asked, hurrying after them. *Horrible day to wear a tight skirt.* She cursed her fashion decision but somehow kept up with their long strides.

"Miss, you need to stay here," a nurse with yellow scrubs informed her, holding up her hands.

Joci watched Adrian and the paramedics disappear through the doors with Medical Personnel Only written on them in bright red letters.

"Yeah, sure. Can somebody keep me updated?"

The nurse squeezed Joci's hand. "You bet. I'll come check on you in a bit, okay?"

She nodded, and the nurse vanished through the same doors. For one long minute, Joci stood outside the double doors and peered through the glass. Even after Adrian's gurney turned down another hall, she couldn't move. Her mind flashed to the last time she was in a hospital. It had been a happier time. *Well, most of it.*

That was the day Adrian had left her alone with a newborn. She swallowed at the flummoxing memories. In one regard, she understood his need to get his mind right. But she couldn't forget the abandonment. It stung, no matter how much time passed.

Looking around, she saw the sign for the waiting room. Her knees knocked together, so she headed that direction. *I need to sit.*

She found an open spot and wracked her mind. He'd acted fine during the trial, no glimmer of an issue until the end. Biting her thumbnail, she kept reviewing but came up short. It wasn't abnormal for an attorney to be a little clammy during court, so she hadn't worried about him. *But you weren't exactly watching him, were you?* She rested her elbows on her knees and ran her hands through her hair. *What will happen if Adrian dies?* She closed her eyes. *For real, this time.*

She rubbed her hands together, glancing at the double doors every few minutes. Imagining a life without Adrian was something she'd done before. *More than once.* While she was still mad at him for his mob involvement, she couldn't wish death on him. He was Brett's dad, for better or worse.

She wouldn't go so far as to say she forgave him, but after watching him with her sons and attending therapy with him, she understood him a little better. Losing Adrian now would definitively leave her questioning everything he'd done over the last two years. She needed to know it all. *He better live long enough to explain.*

She pulled out her phone and gasped at the time. Returning to court today would be impossible. She sent a few text messages and tapped her shoes against the floor, waiting on replies.

Joci: Can you cover my hearing in fifteen minutes?
Rayna: You bet. Why?
Joci: Adrian collapsed after trial. I'm at the hospital.
Rayna: Holy shit. Is he okay?
Joci: Not sure yet. He coded when we arrived. I'll let you know.

A doctor entered the room, and she held her breath. When he steered toward a family across from her, she let it out. She sent a message to her assistant at Petosa, letting her know they wouldn't be back today. The woman promptly replied and promised to update the firm.

The doors slid open, but the two nurses headed toward the hallway that led to billing, so she sent another text.

Joci: Don't freak out, but I'm at the hospital with Adrian.

Instead of replying, Cameron called.

"Hey, I'm fine. Adrian just collapsed after trial," she explained before he could get a word in.

"O'Brien called and filled me in."

"Right, of course. I forgot you knew him." She stared at her shoes. "Is he part of the—"

"I couldn't tell you that even if I knew, Joce." He cleared his throat. "But I'll just say this: he's Irish, not Italian."

"You mean—"

"Any update about Adrian's status?" Cameron cut in.

"Not yet. I'm sure someone will be out soon to let me know."

The siren went off on the other end of the line, and she flinched at the loud sound. It normally didn't bother her, but it did then and there.

"I gotta go, babe. Quinn's pedal-happy foot is chasing down a car. I'll call you later."

Joci heard Quinn yell something in the background, but the call dropped before she could decipher it. Checking her office email, she noticed several new potential cases. She scrolled past them, marking them to read later. One email stuck out amid the notifications. Opening it, she scanned the contents.

Ms. Dorous,

The board has reviewed your recent proposal regarding dissolution of your partnership. At this time, we cannot advise our shareholders to allow this. Your expertise is too important, and the late Brett Petosa wouldn't approve of your departure. At the end of the year, should you still wish to leave Petosa Law P.C., we will reevaluate your request.

She narrowed her gaze and let out a sigh. That was her last attempt at getting out. At least for the time being. Her in-person plea at the last board meeting didn't go well, but she'd hoped a written request would bode better. *So much for that.* She was stuck. Until she could figure a way out.

"Mrs. Petosa?"

She winced at the name. Lifting her gaze, she met the eyes of a short woman and stood. "It's Dorous. I was never— Never mind. How's Adrian?"

"I'm Dr. Scott." She tapped on the tablet in her hands. "The shrapnel in Adrian's chest moved closer to his heart, which caused him to pass out. We got his heart started again, but we need to operate."

Joci nodded, recalling the conversation she had with him about it last year. "You have to remove it? Won't that be difficult?"

"Extremely, but I'm confident in my team." Dr. Scott

turned the tablet around. "These are his most recent scans from two months ago. We're getting new ones to see where exactly all the shrapnel gravitated to, but this is extensive damage."

The moment she looked at the screen, Joci wanted to cry. Black dots were scattered along his torso. The one closest to his heart was the biggest out of all of them. "He said there were only a few."

"He probably didn't want to worry you." Dr. Scott frowned. "Though, with this type of damage, I would've said something. Have you gone to other appointments with him?"

"No. He's my ex-husband." She shifted on her feet, her toes suddenly pinched in the heels. "He's told me very little about his injuries."

"Well, you're listed as his medical power of attorney and emergency contact."

Joci shrugged. "I'm not surprised. Adrian doesn't update information very often, but I'm not the person who should be making these decisions."

Dr. Scott focused on the tablet. "Well, you're listed, and unless we can get in touch with Brett Petosa, you're it."

She rubbed her temple, silently cursing her luck. "Brett's his dad. He died last year."

"Oh, I see."

They stood in silence until Joci asked, "What do you need from me?"

"A signature for the surgery, since Adrian can't consent."

The doctor tapped on the screen until a box appeared.

"And you're positive you can get it all and not kill him in the process?" Joci searched the woman's almond-colored eyes.

"I wouldn't try if I couldn't," Dr. Scott replied. "I was an Army surgeon before returning to Iowa. I've seen and removed my fair share of shrapnel, believe me."

Knowing she didn't have any other choice, Joci used her finger to scribble her name. "How long will it take?"

"It could be an hour, it could be five." Dr. Scott offered her an understanding smile. "If you want to leave, I'll call once we're out of surgery."

"Thanks. I might do that."

"Not a problem. I'll see you later," Dr. Scott said, then took off toward the operating rooms.

She didn't like the idea of leaving Adrian all alone, but she couldn't stay either. Staying meant he was someone important to her, and she didn't want to admit that. He had been, but in the past.

She gathered her purse and then remembered she didn't have a car. Grabbing her phone, she dialed Cameron.

"Hey, can you pick me up?"

"Already on top of it," he replied with a chuckle.

"You are?"

"Walk outside and find out."

Hanging up, Joci moved toward the exit. She recognized the police car waiting outside the emergency bay.

Cameron got out of the car and jogged over to her.

"Damn, you must be freezing," he said, taking off his heavy coat and covering her shoulders with it.

"Thanks."

He pulled her close and searched her eyes. "Are you okay? I'm sure it was scary for you."

She leaned her forehead against his. "It was, but I'm all right."

His arms encircled her until she was pressed against his solid chest. "C'mon, let's get in the car before we turn into snowmen."

Joci noticed the snow accumulating on his head and laughed. They hurried toward the SUV and climbed in the back seat. "Hey, Quinn."

Quinn turned around and gave her a cheeky smile. "Hey, Joci." He pointed at his partner and cocked his brow. "Don't get any ideas back there."

Cameron smirked and rolled his eyes, tucking her next to him. "Wouldn't dream of giving you a show."

The drive home went faster than she hoped. Being alone wasn't something she wanted just then. All she craved was curling up in Cameron's arms until she found out Adrian's fate. She unlocked the door and waved to Quinn before stepping inside. The scent of citrus reminded her the cleaning company was there.

"Do you want me to leave work early?" Cameron asked, standing in the entryway. "We can head to the hospital after I get back if you want."

Joci set down her purse and glanced to the clock on the wall. The twins were midnap, and their nanny was running around the house somewhere. *Probably watching Maria and her crew.* It was one of her not-so-friendly habits, according to the woman who came to the house twice a month to deep clean.

She slipped off her heels. "That'd be great, actually, if you don't mind. I don't really want to go back, but I feel like it's my responsibility as his power of attorney."

Cameron stepped over and gently kissed her. "I get it. Be back soon." He kissed her again, then retrieved his coat.

Once the door shut, she shivered. Whether from missing Cameron's warmth or the events of the day, she didn't know. What she did know was that discovering more about what happened during Adrian's absence was much higher on her to-do list.

CHAPTER SEVEN

The hospital smelled the same as Cameron remembered. Walking through the lobby, he smiled at the woman in the gift shop. The staff tried to make people feel welcome, but he doubted a hospital would ever be a place he'd want to visit. Levi sang from his car seat. *Well, except for meeting these guys.* He looked over at Brett in the seat in his left hand. The redhead was slowly waking from the nap the car ride had lulled him into. Levi never slept in the car, but Brett did every time.

Joci stopped and asked the receptionist for Adrian's room information. The surgeon had called an hour ago, letting them know Adrian was out of surgery and in recovery. Now, he was here to support Joci. That was it. *I'd be completely fine if Adrian left again.*

Brett started crying, and Cameron cursed himself for his thought. He was vindictive, but he'd never be okay with a kid not knowing his dad. That wasn't a life for anyone. While his dad barely cared about him, the same couldn't be said about Adrian. He rocked the car seat, and Brett's crying ceased, and his eyes closed once more.

"He's on the second floor," Joci stated, returning to him.

Cameron had to admit, she looked calmer this go around. When he'd picked her up a few hours ago, she'd been frazzled. She still seemed nervous but better than earlier. The time in-between seemed to help somewhat.

"Great, do you want to go up alone first or…." He let the rest hang there. Joci was aware of his feelings toward Adrian.

Her hazel eyes dimmed for a split second. "I guess I can."

Dammit. She sounded sad, and he couldn't have that. He picked up the twins and shook his head. "Why don't we go with you? I'm sure Adrian will want to see Brett if he's awake."

Her lips curved into a smile. "Good idea."

"Lead the way, counselor."

He followed her toward the elevators, then hit the button for the second floor once they piled inside.

"You know, I can carry one of the boys," she suggested.

He waved aside her offer and did an arm curl with the car seats before he placed them on the floor. "Nah, they're my arm workout for the afternoon."

"Yeah, because you totally need an arm workout." She rolled her gorgeous eyes, and he couldn't stop himself from kissing her. She was the queen at eye rolls, but he didn't mind. He knew the surefire way to make her stop.

"What was that for?" she asked, breathless, when he pulled back.

"Just wanted to kiss you." He tucked her hair behind her ears. "That okay with you?"

"Always."

The elevator dinged, their arrival imminent. "Good, because I like kissing you." He picked up the boys. "Let's do this."

Joci laughed, then grinned at the person waiting for them to leave the elevator. Cameron took a breath and tried not to watch her ass sashay away from him. He couldn't help it. Not when her blue plaid leggings practically begged for his attention.

"Here it is," she said after they wove through the white hallways. He'd never admit it out loud, but hospitals gave him the creeps.

She met his gaze. "You ready for this? Dr. Scott said he may be groggy for a while, so I don't know what to expect. He might be an asshole."

"Won't know until we go in." He watched her struggle between opening the door and leaving it closed. She didn't have to tell him she was wary of the outcome. It was written on her face.

Joci finally turned the handle and strode into the room, her shoulders straight and head high. It was partly why Cameron loved her. She confidently faced whatever came her way. It was damn sexy too.

"I think he's sleeping," she said, peeking at the hospital bed.

Cameron placed the car seats on the two empty chairs and

joined her. Looking down, he noticed Adrian didn't move beneath the white sheets. It truly was a pity the hospital didn't have a better color. The man was pale enough without having the sheets make him look worse.

"Looks like." Levi started fussing from the seat. "I'm going to take him out. He isn't fond of being cooped up."

Joci glanced over to him. "Like father, like son."

He chuckled and retrieved his son. "We like our space, don't we, Levi?" He held up the baby, who grinned cheekily.

"You two are trouble." She smirked and pulled up a chair next to the bed.

Cameron noticed she smoothed the blanket over Adrian and was relieved when she stopped at that. The man didn't deserve her gentle touch after all he'd done. Walking to the window, he pulled back the blind and hoisted Levi up to see outside. The baby merely stared out into the snowy world, his brown eyes large saucers.

"Joci?" Adrian rasped, catching Cameron's attention. He turned in time to see Adrian grip her hand.

"Hey, you gave us a scare." She withdrew her hand and offered a small smile. "How're you feeling?"

Adrian tried to sit up, and pain flashed on his face. "Not very good."

"I'll call for the doctor," Cameron suggested, moving to the door. He didn't wait for either of them to respond. Checking on Brett, he saw the baby starting to wake up again, so he quickly left the room and scanned the hallway.

"Can we get a doctor in here?" he asked the first person he saw. "The patient is awake."

The woman in scrubs merely nodded and scurried toward the nurses' station. A moment later, he heard the call over the speaker system for a doctor to Adrian's room.

Job now complete, he hurried back to see Joci holding a still groggy Brett up on the edge of the bed. Adrian slowly reached over and grazed his fingers over the baby's leg, an emotional expression on his face.

Just for a moment, Cameron put himself in Adrian's shoes. While he swore to never do anything to hurt his family, he realized it was always a possibility that might happen while he remained in the Del Rossi mob. He'd relish any contact Joci gave him with their son, the same as Adrian. Watching, Cameron had never felt more out of place.

"He's so big," Adrian commented.

"You saw him last week." Joci laughed, tickling Brett under his arms. The baby giggled and kicked his feet.

"True, but I'm positive this guy grew since then." He tried to sit up again, then shook his head. "Guess I'm not supposed to move."

"No, you're not," a woman's voice scolded. Cameron swore softly under his breath. He'd been so focused on the interaction that he hadn't heard her come in, and that wasn't normal for him. *Domestic life is turning me soft.*

"Dr. Scott, good to see you again," Joci said, standing and putting Brett on her hip.

"Surgery took longer than I anticipated, but overall everything went well." The doctor walked over to Adrian. After checking his stats, she updated his information on the tablet she held. "We got all the shrapnel out." She smiled.

"Even the pieces near his vital organs."

"That's good, then." Joci glanced to Adrian, then back to the doctor. "Right?"

Dr. Scott nodded. "Yes, very. We have Adrian on several antibiotics to keep infection away. That will be the real issue for the next few days." She looked to Adrian. "If everything goes as planned, we can release you by the weekend."

"Okay, and when can I sit up?" Adrian asked, looking at his son. "I want to be able to hold that handsome redhead."

The doctor hit a button that elevated the back of the bed. "That solves your first problem." She walked around the bed and smiled at Brett. "As for your miniature lookalike, I'd like contact to remain minimal. Any sudden movements may disrupt the healing, and this little guy looks like a mover."

Adrian's face fell. "When, then?"

Dr. Scott patted his shoulder reassuringly. "Small steps first. If you aren't in pain and you're taking care of the incisions, you'll know when you can return to your normal self." She turned to Joci. "Will you be around to help out?"

"Oh, um, well…." Joci fumbled for words. It made sense to Cameron why the doctor would assume, but it also irked him. She'd told him she set the hospital staff straight about their relationship. He immediately wondered if Adrian had put Dr. Scott up to it.

"Joci has plenty to worry about other than me," Adrian said. "I'll hire a nurse to drop in now and then."

Seemingly appeased by the answer, Dr. Scott gave Adrian a few more instructions, then left with a smile.

Brett started whining, and Joci did her best to calm him. The normal techniques didn't work, so Cameron carefully switched Levi with Brett.

"Thanks, he likes you more than me sometimes," she said with a laugh.

The baby quieted after a moment, and Cameron looked over to see Adrian watching them closely. "Glad you're on the road to recovery," Cameron said, hoping to wipe the scowl off the other man's face.

Adrian shifted on the bed. "Thanks, me too."

Cameron's phone buzzed from his pocket, and when he pulled it out, he frowned.

Bambi: GET OVER HERE NOW.

He shoved it back in his pocket, not responding. The fact that it was in all caps only furthered his decision. Dealing with any Del Rossi business wasn't on his docket for the evening. He'd done his part. Now he was waiting for the exchange, which would happen in two days. Discussing anything further with Jerry or Bambi wasn't necessary. He'd avoid them both if it came to it.

Joci and Adrian chatted about work, and Cameron's phone vibrated again.

Bambi: You have an hour. If you aren't here, we'll pay Adrian a visit first. I don't think he'd put up much of a struggle if I smothered him, do you?

The context made him clench his jaw. It was just like her to manipulate by using more than one person as her pawn.

"We'll let you get some rest and come visit tomorrow," Joci said fifteen minutes later.

Cameron bundled the twins into their carriers, fully ready to be done with the hospital and Adrian for the day. If he hadn't insisted on coming with Joci, he wouldn't have been there. There was still something off about Adrian, and he was eager to discover the truth. No amount of time could make Cameron trust the redheaded attorney again. Not when a part of Adrian would always want Joci for his own.

"Thanks for stopping by. I know it probably wasn't easy for either of you." Adrian looked to Cameron, but he didn't respond. He simply picked up both car seats and walked to the door. Being civil wasn't in his nature when it came to Adrian. He'd tried once, and it ended horribly. He wasn't about to let history repeat itself.

CHAPTER EIGHT

Perusing the screen on her laptop, Joci scrolled through the articles. Each one dealt with brain alterations. After visiting Adrian in the hospital, she was more determined than ever to uncover what had happened to him while under J.J.'s control.

She lifted the mug of coffee to her lips and blew on the hot liquid. Deciding to avoid Petosa Law for the time being, she'd switched her scheduled appointments to meet at her firm with Rayna. Fielding continuous questions about Adrian's recent surgery wasn't how she wanted to spend her time.

Opening an article from a research hospital, she read the variation of testing done on participants in order to better understand how the brain is mapped. Most of it was medical jargon that she skipped over, but she got the gist of what the researchers found. Brainwashing was more than possible, especially when pain was involved in survival.

The dark roast coffee tempted her to take another drink, and she sat back and read the next article about how memory worked, cradling the coffee cup in one hand. Her eyes widened at the testing done on rodents that indeed altered memories. The scientist's conclusion was that the same could be done with humans.

An email popped up in the corner of her screen, and she scrunched her nose. Dealing with needy clients didn't appeal to her at that moment. Joci scrolled to another medical journal website, and a cold shiver ran down her spine. "If therapy techniques are not administered correctly to the patient, disrupting memories can cause irreversible damage." She sighed. "Great. Who knows what that crazy doctor did to Adrian?"

She clicked out of her screen and pulled up the notes she'd jotted while researching. So far, everything pointed to Adrian telling the truth about his time with J.J. It was more than possible to alter someone's memories, if her nearly ten hours of research told her anything.

Still, speaking with a neurologist was next in her search for answers. The appointment for the day after tomorrow glared at her from the sticky note on her desk. The woman came highly recommended by the hospital where Adrian was currently recovering. Her plan was to meet with the doctor to discuss the effects of his recent surgery, and also sneak in a few questions about his shaky alibi. Her gut warned her not to get involved again, but she needed to know.

"Hey, Joce, your appointment is here," Rayna said from the doorway.

She glanced up and quickly clicked out of her screen. "Okay, thanks. I didn't even hear the bell." She stood and smoothed her navy blue jacket. "I'll be right out."

Rayna pushed her hair out of her eyes. "I was thinking, maybe we should send Adrian some flowers or balloons or something."

"Last I checked, you hated Adrian."

"I do, but I feel a little bad. He's stuck at the hospital with few to no friends and zero family to visit him." Rayna leaned against the doorway. "I mean, he was an ass, but he still deserves someone to care about him."

Joci grabbed a legal pad and pen. "You're right. Even the worst people deserve love." She walked over and hugged her. "Why don't you pick out a few things you like that can be delivered, and I'll check them out when I get done with this client?"

"Sounds good." She turned, but then added, "I don't like him, Joce."

"I know, but you don't have to like someone to be a good person." She grinned. "And you, Rayna Alley, are a very good person."

Rayna rolled her eyes. "Yeah, yeah, I'm awesome. Better hurry up, or your client will think you escaped out the window to avoid him."

"Nah, I only do that when I hear you and Quinn flirting," she teased, which earned her a sly middle finger from her partner. Laughing, Joci walked to the waiting area and braced herself for the last appointment of the day.

***

Clicking the handcuffs in place, Cameron looked over the

perp's shoulder and watched Quinn tackle the accomplice. A smirk played over his lips when Quinn hauled the guy up after cuffing him. It didn't hurt that both were covered in slush thanks to the recent heat wave. That was Iowa, though. One day the temperature was well below freezing, and the next, it was time to break out shorts and tank tops.

"You good?" Cameron called, searching the man. A wallet with a driver's license identified his guy as a Francesco Alfonsi of the metro. The Italian names pitched his stomach. *If it smells like shit....*

"I think so" came Quinn's quick reply as he walked his detainee to the squad car. "Dammit."

It was then that Cameron noticed blood on both men. Other than the small scratch on Quinn's jaw, he didn't see pooling anywhere. "Unit 7345 requesting a bus at Euclid and Twelfth Street."

"Copy that, 7345. Bus en route," dispatch replied.

Cameron safely stowed his guy in the back seat and ran around the car to relieve Quinn. "Whose blood is it?"

Quinn eyed the crimson liquid on his arm and rolled up his sleeve. A deep gash met his view, and he grimaced. "Looks like mine here, but I think I hit him a little hard when I tackled him. Pretty sure I heard cracking."

Holding in a chuckle, Cameron thoroughly searched the man, who'd been caught breaking into a thrift store with his buddy. Track marks from repetitive needle injections filled the man's arms and also made Cameron grateful for his gloves.

"Hey, I'm injured here, watch it," the man complained.

"I noticed." Cameron carefully examined the few cuts along the man's legs and face. None appeared bad, but it wouldn't hurt to let the paramedics check him out. He couldn't tell if the older man had been previously wounded or if Quinn truly did hit him a little too hard.

The man twitched when Cameron fished out a small plastic bag filled with a white substance. "And what do we have here? Drugs." He met Quinn's eyes. "Goody."

"I'll let the narcotics division know," Quinn said, returning to the vehicle to make the call.

After pushing the guy against the SUV, Cameron silently assessed the situation. It wasn't uncommon to catch druggies midrobbery, but these two guys looked familiar. "Where's your ID?"

"Must've lost it." The man sniffled. Cameron wrinkled his nose when a breeze drifted the seemingly homeless man's stench to him. That wasn't uncommon either.

"Why a thrift store? There are plenty of other places on the block to choose from that'd have more money."

The man attempted to shrug. "We weren't going for the money." He jerked his head to his accomplice. "His ex-girlfriend donated all his shit here to spite him. Apparently his drugs were hidden in one of the dressers. So we, uh, needed it back."

"Uh-huh." He wasn't buying it. There was more. "What else?"

"Nothin'."

"What's your name?"

"Tim."

Cameron peeked into the back seat, then back. The men were a good twenty years apart in age, and the one he arrested wasn't homeless. Far from it, if his clothes were any indicator. He was missing something. The connection.

"All right, Tim, how do you know Francesco?"

Tim coughed, the sound evident of neglected health problems. "He's my dealer."

Nodding, Cameron urged him to explain.

"We met a month ago. Francesco lets me trade for my drugs. This time when I needed a fix, Francesco said I had to help him retrieve a few personal items."

"In the thrift store."

"Yeah, like I said, his girl kicked him out and donated his shit."

A break in the clouds made Cameron squint. "Who does Francesco work for?"

Tim shrugged. "I don't know, man. He talks Italian sometimes when I pick up my goods. I don't ask questions. I live by the river, so I do whatever he wants for free drugs."

Pain snaked its way up Cameron's chest. Coincidences weren't that common. Not when they involved an Italian drug dealer. He'd never dealt with any Del Rossis during his time as a police officer, mostly because he told Jerry the places officers looked for drug exchanges and if any detectives were on their scent. *Shit, they fucked up this time.*

"What were you supposed to steal?"

"An antique dresser. No big deal."

"Stay put," he commanded. There was one surefire way to find out if Francesco was Del Rossi. No one faced potential jail time for an empty dresser.

Quinn hopped out of the driver seat when Cameron opened the back door. "Watch Tim, will you?"

"Sure, no problem. What're you looking for?"

Cameron shoved up Francesco's left sleeve until he saw it. In black-and-white lettering, a bold D and R sat among black ivy. It was Del Rossi's mandatory tattoo. "Shit."

"What?"

Glaring at Francesco, he cursed again, this time in Italian, and continued on in the same language. "You idiot. Jerry is going to be pissed you got caught. What's in the dresser?"

"My client list in Iowa. Plenty of businessmen on that list too." Francesco chuckled. "You must be the inside man. It'll be fine. Jerry will take care of me."

"Yeah, because he's so good at that."

"Be a friend and grab the list before the detectives get here, yeah?"

"Screw off." Cameron quickly slammed the back door and stared at the small crowd that had gathered since the arrest. The wail of an ambulance was close now, and he couldn't wait to be rid of the Del Rossi drug pusher. Francesco expected him to help sweep the arrest under the rug. Unfortunately, he didn't have much of a choice. *Yet.*

"You want to explain what just happened there?" Quinn asked, the ambulance pulling into the parking lot.

He met his partner's curious green eyes. "Not really, no."

"Del Rossi?"

"Yep."

"Shit." Quinn waved at the paramedics. The two men

quickly got to work on Tim, leaving the officers to finish up with their initial paperwork.

By the time they dropped both off at the station, Cameron had texted Jerry and advised him of the situation. He normally didn't have to get this involved in Del Rossi business. Jerry took care of his people. Well, in his own way. Regardless, if one of his people was arrested, the mobster knew about it and usually had bail money on its way. Cameron's role was to keep Jerry up-to-date on the police department. That was it. *Until today.*

Once shift was over, Cameron showered in the locker room and then simply sat on the bench and stared at the floor. Jerry was testing him. His boss had demanded Francesco's charges be dropped. Cameron didn't have that kind of power, not by himself. He didn't want to involve Joci and wouldn't if he could help it. Francesco would be released later today anyhow.

He ran his fingers through his damp hair. What really kicked him was the news that Francesco wasn't Del Rossi's usual drug dealer in the metro. He came to town a month ago. With Bambi. She was slowly ruining his life, and there wasn't much he could do about it. *Not until I'm out.*

***

"Joci, come in," the slender doctor said with a polite smile.

"Thanks for meeting with me, Dr. Macro. I understand you're the best neurologist in Iowa."

"As my colleagues like to tease, I'm the best Macro with the micro." She laughed at her own joke.

"I'm sure you are." Joci crossed her left leg over her right knee. "I was hoping you could explain a little about my ex-husband's condition."

Dr. Macro pulled off her cap dotted with kittens and nodded. "Of course. Mr. Petosa signed a release for you to discuss his charts with me." She scooted up to the desk and clicked her mouse a few times before turning the screen. "As you can see, Adrian's latest MRI scans show traumatic brain injury." She enhanced the photo. "From my review, it appears this trauma occurred in the last year."

Joci squinted at the side-by-side scans. It was odd to study anyone's brain, much less the man's she was once married to. "What would cause this?"

"Well, I've seen Adrian's full file, so I know he was in a car accident and held against his will for several months." Her brows furrowed. "If I had to make an educated guess, either of those events."

"Then—"

"I don't believe Adrian was cared for, medically, that is." She clicked to a new set of scans. "The trauma to his body is seen in his scarring, but the neurological disadvantages of continued trauma are evident in these." She pulled up a new scan and put them next to each other. "The one on the left is Adrian three years ago during his yearly exam. His brain and all functions are typical for a man his age. The scan on the right is from a day ago." She used the mouse to circle the differences. "I don't want to get too technical on you, but his brain tissue was torn at one point, and you can see how it healed."

"Sure." She reviewed the screen again, then asked, "Is it possible to brainwash someone?"

Dr. Macro nodded. "Yes, definitely."

"And memory problems…, is that typical in that form of torture?"

She sat back slightly and pursed her lips. "It is, although every person reacts differently to brain manipulation."

"And in your professional opinion, do you believe Adrian Petosa's mind was altered in any way?" Joci cringed when the doctor's brows lifted at her questioning. "Sorry, I'm an attorney. It's difficult to turn off sometimes."

"No problem, most people aren't so prepared." She smiled. "Over the years, I've encountered more brain scans than I can count. Adrian's images are similar to those found in people suffering from PTSD."

"Do you think he's a danger to me or our son?" she asked in a small voice. It wasn't what she wanted to air, but she needed to hear the words from a professional.

Dr. Macro folded her hands on the desk and offered her a sympathetic smile. "I can't make that determination, Joci. A psychologist or therapist would be more appropriate to answer. I study the brain and what happens when trauma occurs. It's different for each person. I'm sorry I can't be of more help."

"No, that's fine." She stood and shook the doctor's hand. "You've been very helpful. Thank you again for meeting with me."

"Anytime."

Joci left the office and leaned against the wall once the

doctor closed the door. While informative, she couldn't make a complete decision about Adrian. Not until she did more research. *Maybe I can find similar cases.* She sighed. *At least I know he's not making it up.*

She watched a nurse wheel a patient down the hallway. No matter how many times she visited the hospital, a part of her never wanted to walk through the doors again. *Maybe I should switch hospitals.*

Checking her cell phone, she swiped away the missed call from Rayna. She'd talk to her in the morning about her little neuro meeting. Ambling down the hallway, Joci paused outside Adrian's room. She hadn't planned on visiting him, but she was there and he had no one.

She cautiously opened the door. *Please be asleep.*

"Joci, hi."

Or not. She smiled and stepped inside. "Hey, how're you doing?"

Adrian motioned to his dinner of what looked like beef and noodles. To her, it looked disgusting. "Other than wishing I ordered a pizza?"

Smirking, she sat in the chair beside his bed. "There's still time for that."

"Nah, the doc will have my ass if I deviate from her nutrition plan." He pushed away the tray. "What're you doing here?"

"Would you believe hunting for clients?"

He shook his head. "Not even for a second."

"Darn, had to try." She fidgeted in the seat, staring at her red heels.

"You weren't here for me, were you?"

This made her look up. A cocky smile played on his face, and she rolled her eyes. "Don't act so surprised. You're important to my life. Brett's life."

"Right." He held up his cell phone. "You could've texted me to see how I was."

"True, but I was already here." He sipped his water and motioned for her to continue. "I met with Dr. Macro."

"Ah."

"She told me quite a few things." Joci searched his face for any indicators of deceit or worry, but none presented.

"Anything I should know? It was my brain you were discussing, was it not?"

"It was, but no, nothing to report that you don't already know."

Adrian nodded once and focused on the television across the room. For a few minutes, Joci tried to decipher why she was even still there. They had nothing more to discuss, and it wasn't the rerun of *Friends* that kept her from leaving. It was Adrian. But she didn't want to talk about the last year. She wanted it to disappear.

"If you're going to stare at me all night, will you at least stare at the other side of my face? It doesn't have a jagged scar on it."

Joci blinked several times and realized she'd zoned out. Adrian's blue eyes searched hers. A part of her pitied him for being self-conscious. That wasn't the Adrian Petosa she knew. Then again, he was in attorney mode most times she saw him.

"Sorry, I didn't mean to…." She stood and gathered her purse and turned on her toes. "I'll leave you alone."

"That's the last thing I want," he said softly.

"Adrian, I can't do this." Looking over her shoulder, she bit back the urge to yell at him for playing on her emotions.

"I know." He sighed. "I guess I'm just glad you care at all about me."

Joci reached the door and met his gaze. "I do care, Adrian, but not in the way you want."

He forced a smile. "Don't ruin the office while I'm gone, okay?"

Instead of replying, she nodded and closed the door behind her. A short visit with him was all she could handle. *I'm glad he won't be at the office for a few weeks. It'll give me time to figure out a way to leave Petosa.*

She yawned and set off toward the elevator. A glass of wine after the twins were tucked in bed was more than earned after her day.

CHAPTER NINE

Cameron stomped the gray snow from his boots and squinted. The jewel exchange would happen any minute, and he was ready to be done with it all. He'd visited Jerry and Bambi at a local Italian restaurant, and the mob boss had made it clear Cameron was on a tight leash.

Normally he wouldn't mind, since he'd get a nice payday in the end, but this meet was only the first half of his escape from Del Rossi. There was more, and he wasn't entirely sure he wanted to hear it all. Bambi was involved, which meant it was devious and most likely life-threatening.

The shuffling of feet met his ears, and he pushed off the side of the building set to be demolished the next week. A tall, slender man in all gray approached, his ball cap hiding his face. He carried a large duffle bag in one hand, and the other was stuffed in his coat pocket.

"You have the jewels?" the man asked, facing him now.

Cameron shifted on his feet and nodded. "You have the cash?"

"Show me first."

Cameron dug out the velvet bag and poured out two diamonds. He'd done this before. Giving the fence all the loot at once wasn't happening. He'd learned that the hard way when he first started out and got mugged. Jerry thought it was funny, but since then, he'd learned to be smart about exchanges.

The shrewd man grabbed a small magnifying loupe and examined the gems. "They look good," he said after a thorough review. "I have fifty grand as agreed. All small, nonsequential bills."

"Del Rossi said seventy-five thousand," Cameron replied without flinching.

The man smirked and dropped the duffle. "Then it's a good thing I brought that amount, isn't it?"

The hair on Cameron's arms bristled, and an eerie tingle slithered up his spine. *Something isn't right.* While most of his exchanges went smoothly, the fences never carried more than their offer. He had two options: accept the cash, or run before his gut feeling came to fruition.

His phone buzzed, and he swiped away the message from Jerry. He didn't have a choice. If he let his mob boss down, things wouldn't bode well.

Grabbing the duffle's handle, he nodded to the other man and turned on his toes. He needed to hightail it out of the alley.

"Pleasure doing business with you."

The moment the words left the man's lips, Cameron knew he should've left the cash. A spotlight lit up the alley, and a megaphone-enhanced voice echoed in the cramped space.

"Drop the bag and put your hands up," the man shouted.

Muttering every curse word he knew, Cameron did as commanded. He looked over his shoulder to see a slew of FBI officers heading their direction, guns drawn.

"I think we caught the contact for the Del Rossi mob," the supposed fence said, cuffing him.

Cameron chuckled and shook his head. "And I think you just made the biggest mistake of your career, buddy."

"Shut up."

"Okay, okay, go ahead and arrest me. I'll be out before you can wipe your ass from this shit mistake." He laughed when the man roughly pushed him toward the armored car up ahead. His mind spun in different directions, but he knew one surefire way to get out of this situation unscathed. "It isn't every day you catch a police officer undercover, is it?"

Those words made the FBI officer pale. "What? What're you talking about?"

"Book me and find out," Cameron taunted with a sly grin. *So far, so good.* "I hope you enjoy desk duty."

By now, the whole crew of FBI officers surrounded them. The area shone brightly with red, white, and blue lights. It was the one and only time he was grateful he hadn't told Joci where he was heading.

"Stay put," a man with a gruff voice said.

If Cameron could've flipped him off, he would've. This wasn't the first time he'd been cuffed, but it'd been a while since they weren't fur-lined with the promise of Joci's body at the end.

Two men pulled the arresting officer away and spoke

in hushed tones. Every now and then, one of them would look his way, but he didn't budge. Cameron couldn't hear them, but judging from the concerned looks on their faces, his farce was working. He didn't like using his police connections to further Del Rossi, but he sure as hell wasn't about to be thrown back into Polk county jail. Thinking on his feet had come to his rescue more times than not in the mob. It was the sole lesson he thanked Jerry for teaching him at a young age.

After five minutes passed, the arresting officer sauntered back to him.

"We're going to take you to our office until we get this sorted out." He opened the back door of the car and patted him down. Finding Cameron's badge, he lifted his brows. "Hop in, Officer Shearer. I hope you have a good defense attorney."

***

The holding cell wasn't anything he hadn't seen before. Cameron had to admit, it was much nicer than in the county jails he'd frequented in Ohio. They'd uncuffed him upon arrival, though the door remained locked. He could only assume why. They'd call the captain soon enough.

Thirty minutes ticked by before the door opened. He couldn't think about Joci or his boys at the moment. He needed to focus on the case.

"Captain Eicher."

The woman roughly five inches shorter than him pulled out the chair across from him. Instead of sitting in it, she placed her forearms on the back and leaned forward. "So, do you want to fill me in, Shearer, or should I call your actual captain?"

Cameron swallowed hard. He'd given the Feds the wrong information for his superior for a reason. Valeria Eicher had made her career by taking down the biggest mob in New Jersey. She was who he needed in his corner.

"I have a proposition for the station."

"Go on. You already dragged me out of bed, so you might as well spill it."

He wet his lips. "I can give you the Del Rossi mob."

Her dark eyebrows shot up. "That's mighty lofty, given where your ass is right now. How do you expect to hand over Bernard and Bambina?"

"Then you know of them?"

Valeria spun the chair around and sat on it. "It's my job to keep track of the organized crime unit, Shearer, so yes, I know of Del Rossi's presence in Des Moines. What do you have?"

He scratched the top of his ear. "Everything you could ever want. At least, a gateway to it all."

She narrowed her gaze. "How?"

Taking a beat, Cameron meshed his fingers together. If Eicher was on Del Rossi's payroll too, he'd be dead within the hour. "I may or may not be part of Del Rossi." She didn't seem surprised by this, and he instantly panicked. He wasn't as coy as he thought if she was onto him. "For legality's sake, I want immunity for what I've done in the past, present, and future for the mob."

"That can be arranged. How involved are you?"

"Very." Cameron glanced at the clock on the wall. He only had a small amount of time before Joci would show up, fiery and pissed. Giving up the mob wasn't the immediate plan, but it suddenly became very clear that Del Rossi would never let him leave. Not unless he was dead. "When my fiancée arrives, I need you to not say anything."

"Why? Doesn't she—" Valeria paused and nodded. "She doesn't know everything, does she?"

He shook his head. "No, and I'd rather tell her my double role later and not tonight. There'll be enough hell to pay."

Valeria stood. "Fine. I expect you in my office in the morning. The guard will release you after your fiancée has ample time to ream your ass." She smirked. "Gotta give the girl something."

"Thank you, Captain."

"Don't thank me yet. I'm still pissed you woke me up for a sliver of Del Rossi." She knocked on the door, and a guard opened it. "Don't make me regret this."

***

The only word to describe how Joci was feeling was irate. With herself, with Cameron, with the police department. All of them. She slammed the car door and stalked up the stairs to the federal building in Des Moines.

After receiving the call from one of the FBI officers who apprehended Cameron, she'd called Rayna. Thankfully, her friend didn't think twice before hauling herself to watch the boys.

She gripped the handle of the front door and swung it open. The wind caught it, and she winced at the sound it made against the brick exterior. She didn't bother to check in with the night guard. She knew exactly where she was going.

"Ms. Dorous, what brings you here so late at night?" the overnight receptionist asked once Joci entered the holding facility for federal prisoners.

"Hi, Patricia, I'm here to see a client." She buttoned the top button of her coat that just wouldn't stay put. "Cameron Shearer."

"Yeah, they just brought him in." Patricia's face lit up with recognition. "I didn't know he had counsel."

"It's kind of a package deal when you're engaged to one."

The receptionist giggled. "You can go back. They have him in the second cell, but I'm sure one of the officers will talk to you first."

Joci thanked her and went through the locked door once it buzzed open. Normally, there were ropes to cross and forms to sign, but the Feds hadn't arrested Cameron, just detained him. There was no reason to keep him. At least, she hoped there wasn't.

"Joci, this is a surprise," Agent Stevens said, greeting her in the hallway.

She smiled at the seasoned FBI team leader. "Hey, Stevens. I'm here to see—"

"Shearer. I know." He jerked his head. "C'mon, he hasn't said a word since asking someone to call you."

"Why's he here?"

They reached another door, and only after he used his key card to enter did he answer. "We caught him making a jewel exchange. Diamonds, to be exact. The fence originally meant for him was incarcerated this morning, so we decided to keep the appointment and see what fish we could reel in." He stopped outside of another door. "We weren't expecting Del Rossi involvement."

Joci peeked into the small window of the holding cell. It was homier than the county jail, and Cameron was alone, lying on the bed and staring at the ceiling with one leg propped up on the other knee.

"But your client said he's undercover with the DMPD."

She blinked several times. *Surely, he would've told me.* She shifted her weight. Not telling her would make sense too. "It's a possibility, yes."

Stevens unlocked the door. "We're still checking on that, but you can go in and talk. We turned off the cameras. I'll let you know when we hear back from his captain."

"Thanks, Stevens." She waited until the man walked in the other direction before pulling open the door and entering the small room.

Cameron's eyes dipped from the popcorn-textured ceiling until they rested on her. "Hey, babe."

She tilted her head to the left. "'Hey, babe' is all I'm getting for coming down here at ten at night?" She tossed her purse to the bed and propped her hands on her hips.

"It's a misunderstanding, plain and simple." He stood and reached for her, but she backed up.

"A misunderstanding, huh? Well, then why don't you explain it to me?" She watched him closely for a reaction. Seeing him in a cell again brought back all the memories from the last time. He wasn't an asshat like back then, but he was still as cocky, if not more so. It shouldn't have been attractive, but the way he pushed back his hair only to have it flop back in his eyes was wearing down her wrath.

Scratching his chin, he glanced to the door behind her. "I was undercover."

"Bullshit."

He smirked. "That's my story."

"And you're sticking with it?" she finished, scowling.

"One hundred percent."

He retreated to the bed and plopped down again. This was all familiar to him. He'd been locked up many times before, and he wasn't worried. He was never worried about being locked away. She folded her arms over her chest and stared at him.

"Jerry put you up to this, didn't he? He's the reason you're in this mess."

"I'd like to say no...."

"But you can't." She swept her hair back into a ponytail and adjusted her glasses. "Want to tell me the truth now?"

"I can't." His brown eyes avoided her gaze. "You know that, Joce."

He looked too comfortable with his back against the wall and legs crossed at the ankles on top of the bed. There wasn't a scrape on him from what she could tell. The tattoos peeking out from his shirt reiterated his past and instantly reminded her of the unknown parts of him.

It hit her then that he'd never be afraid to go to prison or jail. He had a get-out-of-jail-free card. *Two, actually.* Del Rossi and her. Both would stop at nothing until he was exonerated. She'd witnessed it firsthand during his murder trial.

"If you want to come home, you'll tell me."

Cameron's right eye twitched, and the boyish grin slipped off his face. "You're seriously giving me an ultimatum?"

She cleared her throat. "In a way, yes. I can't be in the dark anymore, Cam. It isn't fair to our relationship or our kids. I already worry you won't come home because of your day job." She waved to the room. "Now this has me concerned about you coming home in general because of the mafia."

He moved to the edge of the bed and looked over to her. "Can I tell you when we get home?"

"No. Now."

He sighed and patted the spot next to him. "All right." She took a seat and leaned closer when he lowered his voice. "I was moving some jewels that Bambi and I stole."

"You said—"

"I know what I said, but I don't have a choice. Once I'm done with these jobs, I'm out." His eyes searched her face. "As in done with Del Rossi. For real this time."

Joci caught her bottom lip between her teeth. She'd heard this before. "What else do you have to do?"

He laced her hand with his and squeezed once. "I don't know. Jerry's keeping it hush-hush for obvious reasons."

She thought it over. The mobster would use whatever weapon was at his disposal to destroy Cameron should he refuse the work. It didn't sit right in her stomach. The hope that they could have a life outside of the mob was the only reason she didn't argue with him.

"Can you promise me you aren't returning to a full-time mobster life and merely lying to appease me?"

A sad smile crept over his face. Cupping her jaw in his hands, he pinned her with his intense brown gaze. "I swear on my life, Joce. All I want is out. This is the way."

She searched his hopeful eyes. He was a good liar, but not when it came to her. "I believe you."

He lightly kissed her lips. "That means more than you know."

Joci leaned into him and nestled her face against his neck. Her emotions, while still riddled with havoc, calmed for the moment. She trusted him with her future. She didn't want it any other way. If this was how they'd have one together, then she'd help him get there.

"All right, Shearer, you're free to go," Agent Stevens said from the doorway.

They both looked over at the FBI agent. Joci stood first, grabbing Cameron's hand on her way up.

"Any charges?"

Stevens shook his head. "No." He looked to Cameron. "Your captain wants to talk to you in the morning, though."

Cameron nodded once. "Sure. Thanks." He slipped by Stevens, not giving the man another second of his time.

Joci followed close behind, thanking the agent as they

left. She looked over at the man beside her. Life with Cameron was anything but dull. She just hoped it'd be a long life.

CHAPTER TEN

It's been one hell of a month. Cameron opened the front door and frowned when darkness greeted him. It was late, but Joci usually left on the light over the kitchen sink to welcome him after a grueling shift.

He kicked off his boots and rubbed his eyes, yawning as he walked toward the living room. Falling into bed was his first priority. *And cuddling next to Joci*. That was a close second.

After chasing a man high on meth for twelve blocks, he'd hoped the shift would improve. Unfortunately, he and Quinn were busy the entire time and barely had a break to eat sub sandwiches between calls.

Cracking his neck, he made it to the hallway before a dark voice met his ears.

"What do they know, Cameroni?"

"Shit," he hissed, turning around quickly. If he hadn't recognized the voice, he would've pulled his gun too. But this one he knew too well. He flipped on the light, and Jerry Del Rossi came into view. Sitting in the recliner with fingers steepled, the mob boss didn't fit among the toys strewn along the neighboring couch.

"I wasn't expecting anyone this late." Cameron cleared his throat and glanced around the room. They weren't alone. Jerry didn't go anywhere without at least three bodyguards. As to where the men were hidden, he almost didn't want to know. Immediately, thoughts of a sleeping Joci and twin boys made his heart race. *What if they're in trouble?*

"They're fine, don't worry," Jerry said, as if hearing his thoughts.

He wouldn't believe his boss even if the man swore on a Bible. Shifting his weight, Cameron crossed his arms over his chest.

"What're you doing here?"

Standing, the short man walked to the mantle and reviewed the framed photos. "You truly have a beautiful family." He traced a heart-shaped frame with a photo of Cameron and Joci in it. "A stunning fiancée and two boys who adore you." Jerry turned his neck to meet Cameron's gaze. "It would be a pity if you did something to jeopardize their lives."

Cameron's body tensed even more. "I didn't tell the police anything."

"Police, I can handle." Jerry adjusted one of the frames that was facing the wrong direction. "I'm more concerned with the Federal agents you spoke with." His bushy brows rose. "Anything to tell me?"

He swallowed hard. Of course, Del Rossi had him followed. "They don't know anything either."

"Then why aren't you in prison? I have it on good authority you were caught with my cash and diamonds."

The holstered gun at Cameron's side suddenly seemed too good to pass up, but he couldn't shoot. Not only would it endanger his family, but it'd also tip his hand to Del Rossi. Even if he managed to kill Jerry, the mobster's siblings would come after him and anyone associated with him.

"I have some connections from being on the force and through Joci." He shoved his hands in his pants pockets. "They don't know anything. I played it off as trying to catch a fence."

Jerry's dark eyes bored into Cameron, and he kept the connection, hating it the entire time. His Italian boss liked eye contact until it was uncomfortable. A good old-fashioned staring contest was one of Jerry's techniques to see if a person was lying.

After a few minutes, a grin covered Jerry's face and he closed the distance between them. "You're one of a kind, Shearer." He clapped Cameron's shoulder and nodded. "I'll be in touch."

Before Cameron could revel in his victory, Jerry added, "I'm always watching. Don't forget that." The door closed softly, a breath of cold air filling the room.

Cameron kept his eyes glued to the chair Jerry had recently vacated. If he could toss the thing into the street and douse it with gasoline and a match, he would. The fact that Del Rossi had broken into his house while his family slept meant they didn't trust him. *Not like they used to.*

He let out a frustrated breath and stalked over to the

front door. He peered through the small window. Only darkness met him. Any sliver of Jerry's existence had already dissipated into the dark night. Cameron turned the lock and decided they needed to add a few more security devices to the house. His mob protection couldn't be trusted anymore.

He double-checked the locks and windows before finally heading toward the bedrooms. Once he saw Brett and Levi safely slumbering, he closed their door and slipped into the master bedroom.

Standing at the end of the bed, he watched Joci's chest rise and fall gently. A content expression lined her lips, and he roughly ran both hands over his face. He gripped the edge of the bed frame. *Jerry could've killed them while they slept.* His hands suddenly shook. *This is getting out of control.* He'd known his decision to involve the police and FBI was the right one, but now he was increasingly wary of the outcome.

Shedding his uniform, Cameron slipped beneath the sheets and nestled Joci against him. He inhaled, and the familiar scent of fresh berries made him smile despite the circumstances.

I can't lose her. I can't lose any of them. He gently kissed her shoulder and closed his eyes. Getting out of the mob was always his endgame, even more so since he reconnected with Joci. More lives were at stake, and he couldn't let them down.

"I'll do whatever it takes to keep you safe."

***

Twenty children raced around the indoor playground, excited screams filling the air. Joci sat beside her boys as they played in the miniature ball pit. Normally, she'd wait until the boys could participate more, but they'd been invited to the birthday party of the child of one of Joci's oldest law school friends, and she couldn't refuse.

"Joce, so glad you could make it," Jeremy Schroeder said, walking over. On his left hip sat a brown-eyed beauty with ringlet curls. Joci immediately recognized her as Heidi, his middle child and only girl. "I wasn't sure if you would." He sat next to her and placed Heidi next to Brett and Levi. "Wow, they're getting big."

"I was just going to say the same about yours." She craned her neck and spotted his wife, Gwendolyn, with the birthday boy and their newborn.

"Yeah, I still can't believe I have three kids." He smirked. "It's weird. Just when I thought we were done having children, Gwen's pregnant again."

"And of course, you have absolutely nothing to do with that."

Jeremy chuckled, but he couldn't hide the red tint to his cheeks. "They're my everything. I can't imagine life without them."

"Same here." Joci laughed when Brett pulled on Heidi's curls and the girl pushed him away. "Everything going well then with Gwen?"

Jeremy's eyes took on a dreamy state. She'd seen it many times when he spoke about the love of his life. "Oh yeah. We're great." He looked away from his wife. "Did I ever tell you about how we finally ended up together?"

"Not exactly, but I can guess." She grabbed a shiny red ball from Levi's mouth before it could make contact. The last thing she needed were sick twins.

"What about you? You and Cameron going strong?"

"Yep." She laughed. "You know, we've done absolutely zero planning for our wedding. I should probably work on that."

"After how your last marriage ended, I can understand." Jeremy's eyes clouded momentarily. "Is he coming today? I'd like to finally meet him."

"I doubt it." She helped Brett up from being buried in balls. "Being a police officer means he has a crappy work schedule sometimes."

"Sure, makes sense. Plus, who wants to hang out with a bunch of kids who are recently sugared up?"

"Jeremy, can you feed Ian while I get the cupcakes ready?" Gwen asked, walking over.

"You bet." He stood. "Can you watch Heidi for a minute?"

Joci nodded. "No problem."

Jeremy grinned and quickly caught up with his gorgeous wife.

"Looks like it's just us, kiddos," she said, brushing back Levi's hair. It grew faster than Brett's, but both would need haircuts before summer.

"Aw, what adorable children," a woman crooned.

Glancing over, Joci watched a short blonde dressed in a red jumpsuit sit next to Heidi on the edge of the ball pit.

"Thanks." She glanced around. "Is your little guy or girl here for the party?"

The blonde snickered as she brushed back her long hair, and a waft of her perfume met Joci's nose. It was overpowering and expensive, much like the woman's appearance.

Her blue eyes pinned Joci to her seat. Sweat lined her palms even before the other woman spoke. Something wasn't right.

"I'm afraid I'm not a big fan of drooling youth suckers." She held out her hand. "I'm Bambina, by the way. But you can call me Bambi."

Warning bells instantly went off in her mind. *Surely she's not the same Bambi Cameron told me about.* She shook the outstretched hand. "Joci."

"Yeah, Cameroni told me all about you." Bambi snorted, adjusting her bra to expose more cleavage.

"Actually, I take it back. He's told me nothing. I had to find about you on my own."

Panic coursed through Joci's veins. Making a scene wouldn't help matters. She'd wait and see what the woman wanted. *And then call Cam.* She could fight her own battles, but this wasn't one she'd prepared for.

"What do you want, Bambi?"

Bambi crossed her legs and glanced at the three children happily playing. "I want Cameron to do what he's told."

"He knows his place in Del Rossi. He'll do what he's supposed to." She hoped it sounded convincing, because she didn't believe a word of it. Judging from Bambi's expression, she didn't believe her either.

"Yeah, whatever." She leaned over and bopped Brett on the nose. It took every ounce of Joci's restraint to keep from bitch-slapping the blonde. "Your kids are cute. I mean, probably to most people."

Joci sat silently, ignoring the sudden urge to grab both her boys and make a run for it. If she opened her mouth, she might say something she couldn't take back. Cameron had warned her about Bambi's manipulations and how the blonde wasn't beyond physical altercations.

"Tell your cop fiancé to follow his orders." She stood and ruffled Levi's curls. "Or I'll enjoy making him suffer." Bambi's eyes connected briefly with hers, and she let out a dark laugh. "I can't say you'll like it, though."

Holding her breath, Joci watched the woman until she disappeared through the double doors and out of sight. She breathed a sigh of relief that the three toddlers didn't seem fazed by the recent conversation and potential danger. *Hold it together until this is over,* she repeated. She sent Cameron a text but was disappointed when no response chimed.

The birthday song echoed in the distance, and Jeremy came back to grab his daughter before the candles were blown out. Joci moved slower, arms full of Brett and Levi. She stood near the back but didn't join in the festivities. The twins seemed to enjoy the liveliness of the off-tune song, wiggling in her arms until they nearly slipped. She settled them in their high chairs; both were eager to taste the sugary dessert.

Joci dug her phone out of her purse and called Cameron

once the cupcakes were devoured—or in the twins' case, smashed. He didn't answer. *Dammit.* It wasn't uncommon when he was on shift, but in this case, it worried her.

"Everything okay?" Gwen asked, handing her a leftover chocolate cupcake slathered in blue frosting with an edible picture of a truck on top. "You look a little green."

"Yeah, I'm fine." She forced a smile and held up her phone. "Work. It never stops."

Gwen nodded, then returned to the ornery bunch of kids. They stayed to watch the birthday boy open presents, but Brett started fussing as the sugar wore off. They were past due for their naps.

She thanked Gwen and Jeremy, then hurried the boys to the car, turning the heater on full blast. Then and only then did Joci let her emotions free. Tears streaked her mascara until she wore black rims around her eyes. Levi and Brett wailed in the background, and she pushed aside her tears.

"Sorry, boys. I know you're tired, but let's go see Daddy, really quick."

Her words didn't stop their cries—not that she expected it. Turning onto the street, she swallowed her fear and set a path for the police station. She wasn't safe. *No one's safe when the mob's involved.*

***

Throwing the SUV into Park, Cameron cracked his neck, then unbuckled his seat belt. Shift wasn't over, but they had reports to fill out, and the lull in calls had given them the perfect opportunity to return to the station.

"Hey, isn't that Joci's car?" Quinn asked once they made it to the side entrance.

Shielding his eyes from the sun, Cameron spotted the black Mercedes. From the looks of it, no one was inside. "Yep. I wonder what she's doing here."

They walked inside as Quinn teased, "A little afternoon delight?"

Cameron playfully punched his partner. If he was honest, he wouldn't complain in the least if that was why Joci was at the station. They strolled through the open-concept office, cubicles dotted with officers filling out mandatory paperwork. It was his least favorite part of the job.

Coming around the corner to their pair of cubicles, he paused at the sight of Joci and the twins. She sat in the lone chair, both boys on her lap as they read a book. A lump caught in his throat. She was everything he didn't deserve.

Once upon a time, Joci was straight-backed and all business, but that had changed over the last two years. She still kicked ass and took names in court. That would never change. It was one of the qualities that drew him to her in the first place. But she was different now. Softer, even. At least with him.

Joci's hazel eyes lifted at his approach, and he immediately saw something hidden in her gaze. He'd seen it a handful of times, all when danger lurked.

"Counselor, what brings you to our humble workplace?" he asked, grabbing Brett and kissing his cheek.

"Yeah, I thought you had a birthday party," Quinn added, hanging his arms over the side of the cubicle to tickle his namesake's chin.

"I did." She stood and handed the baby to Quinn. "But I ran into someone I didn't particularly like."

Her voice wavered, and Cameron hoped it was simply an awkward run-in with Adrian instead of something more sinister. "Who?"

Joci pushed her glasses up her nose and let out a breath. "Bambi."

Cameron's eyes widened at the same time his cheek twitched. "What?"

"She found me and threatened us." She looked to Levi, who was happily drooling on Quinn, then to Brett, who was snuggling against Cameron's chest. "She—"

"Hang on." He glanced around and lowered his voice. "Let's go into one of the offices." He nodded to Quinn. "You okay with that little guy for a few minutes?"

The officer's green eyes glanced between them playfully at first. His face fell when he didn't see the same emotion on either Cameron's or Joci's face. "Yeah, sure. Everything okay?"

"Not sure yet." Cameron waved for Joci to follow him, then called over his shoulder, "I'll keep you in the loop."

Quinn gave him a curt nod, then returned to fawning over the curly-haired baby in his arms.

They wove through the cubicles until he came across one of the interview rooms. Closing the door behind them, he looked down and noticed Brett had fallen asleep. *This kid never ceases to amaze me.*

Joci stood behind one of the chairs, hands gripping

the back. "She's crazy, Cam."

"Uh-huh." He sat and gently cradled the baby in the crook of his arm. "What exactly did she say?"

"Something about you following orders or she'd enjoy torturing you through me." Her eyes narrowed. "What is she talking about?"

Bambi's brazen act sent a chill down Cameron's spine. If he could get away with murder, she'd be the one person he'd make disappear. Threatening him was one thing, but actually coming face-to-face with his family and threatening to harm them was exactly why he needed to get out of Del Rossi.

"Cameron?"

He leaned back in the chair and studied her long, straight hair that had fallen across her face. Even worried, she was angelic.

"I haven't followed Del Rossi instructions as ordered." He brushed back Brett's hair. "I'm sorry, babe. I didn't think anyone would come near you. It's not acceptable. I'll speak with Jerry about it."

"I'm not worried about Jerry."

"You should be." She frowned, but he kept going. "I'll talk to them. They know how much the three of you mean to me. It's why they're targeting you a second time."

"Wait, second time?" Joci stomped over to him but kept her voice steady. "What else did they do?"

Cameron cringed at the slip. He never should've said anything. Seeing her cross her arms over her chest, he had to come clean. She'd worry herself sick if he didn't. "I came home the other night and Jerry was in our living room."

Her eyes bugged, and she gasped. "What?"

"Shit's getting real. Ever since the FBI got involved, Del Rossi doesn't trust me." He rocked Brett when the baby started whimpering. "I have to take extra precautions from here on in."

"Like what?"

Standing, he pulled her in for a loose side-hug. "Like doing whatever it takes to keep you and the boys safe. I'll speak with the captain about adding a security detail to our house. I'm sure it won't be a problem, given the situation."

Joci buried her face against his shoulder. Her heartbeat pulsed in time with his, and Cameron closed his eyes. He needed Del Rossi out of their lives. Sleeping soundly wouldn't happen again until then.

"I don't like this, Cam."

He kissed the top of her head. "Neither do I."

They stood for a few minutes, neither moving, merely clinging to the unknown future ahead. Finally, Quinn knocked on the door, a crying Levi on the other side.

"I better rescue him," Joci said.

Instead of letting her escape, Cameron gently grabbed the base of her neck and tilted her head up. Enclosing her lips with his, he swallowed her surprise. Joci's hands gripped the front of his shirt, eagerly matching the kiss.

"I love you," he whispered, pulling back slightly.

Her eyes slowly opened, and she smiled. The sight took his breath away more than their recent embrace. "I love you too. Now, don't get killed, okay? I'm not done loving you."

His heart swelled, and he couldn't stop himself from kissing her again. He'd never get enough of her. If this was what people waited their whole lives for, he understood the need entirely.

"Ahem, your child is crying, and I'm pretty sure he left a present in his diaper," Quinn said, interrupting them.

Giggling, Joci patted Cameron's chest once and retrieved Levi. In the disruption, Cameron noticed Brett was no longer sleeping. The blue-eyed wonder lay contently in his arm, having had a front row seat for their kiss.

"Don't worry, little guy, you'll find somebody as awesome as your mom someday," he promised, following Joci and Quinn from the room.

Joci made quick work of Levi's diaper disaster, and Cameron watched the trio pull out of the parking lot before he let the grim details of their visit sink in. He was ready to destroy Del Rossi. They could have him if it came to that, but they'd never have his family.

CHAPTER ELEVEN

Looking over the top of her stack of papers, Joci watched Adrian speak with the court reporter. He acted as though nothing had happened over the last weeks. Well, for him, maybe nothing did. He knew the possibilities of his injuries. Seeing him around the office was still odd. She'd gotten used to being alone. *Well, except for Rayna.*

She highlighted a section of testimony but couldn't focus on the words. Adrian had returned to work last week after being gone for four. No one balked at his missed work, well, because he was the boss. *We both are.*

After Adrian was discharged from the hospital, Joci checked in on him several times at his apartment. Each time, he sent her away, but only after spending time with Brett. She assumed he didn't want her to see him "weak." That was perfectly fine with her. She went for Brett's sake and a little curiosity of her own.

The court attendant laughed at something Adrian said, and Joci flipped to the next page of transcripts. They were waiting for a judge to hear their motion to continue a sentencing, and so far, she'd gotten more work done here than at her office at either firm.

Since her run-in with Bambi, the Des Moines police kept their house under surveillance. She didn't like it, but Del Rossi made their presence known more each day so she didn't mind the friendly shadow from time to time.

Her phone buzzed on the table with a new message.

Quinn: We still meeting for drinks after work?

She picked up the Android and thought out her reply. Quinn was her inside man. Well, one who had been tainted by his friendship with Cameron, but the person she turned to for answers when she worried about her fiancé.

Joci: Yep. Taps 69. See you at 5.

Remembering her partner, she sent another message.

Joci: Hey, want to join Quinn and me for drinks around 6?

She placed the phone back on the table and waited for the reply. It'd come. It always did when booze and Levi Quinn were involved. As for the timing, she needed to speak with Quinn about Cameron without Rayna present. Her best friend was overly protective of her, and if Rayna believed Cameron was up to any misdoings, she'd be the first person to give him the boot.

Rayna: You bet. Order appetizers if you get there before me.

Adrian was chatting with the attendant now, so she pulled out a new file and opened it. *Might as well get more done while I can.* She checked the time and remembered she was scheduled to attend another therapy session with Adrian the next day. This time, the therapist had asked for Cameron not to come. She hadn't liked the idea at first, but Cameron promised to be right outside in the lobby if anything went wrong.

"I think you need a break." Adrian returned to the desk and knocked on it. "You're working hard enough for the both of us."

She chuckled and rifled through the police reports. "Just trying to keep my clients happy."

"Let's grab a coffee from the shop across the street," he suggested. "Nancy said Judge Luther won't be back for a little bit, so we have some time."

"Well, my one cup *is* wearing off...." Weighing the options of getting caffeinated again or wallowing in cases, she stood and slung her purse on her shoulder. "I guess I could take a short break." She grinned. "We better go before the judge decides to come back."

Adrian let the court attendant know where they were headed, and they were off.

"How're you feeling?" she asked when they reached the bottom of the first flight of stairs.

Adrian self-consciously put his hand over his chest. "Better." He smiled over at her. "Thanks for asking."

"We're connected no matter what, Adrian. I'd rather be friendly if we can manage it."

He moved behind her when the oncoming foot traffic overwhelmed their position on the stairs. "Agreed."

Joci tried to keep her distance, but the crowd pushed them closer on their descent. Adrian's familiar Ralph Lauren cologne drifted to her, bringing up memories of the past. She picked up her pace and was clear of the throng before she let herself be sucked into any good thoughts of Adrian.

"You never did like crowds," he commented, catching up to her. He opened the door to the outside world, and she quickly slipped by.

"I like my space when I can get it. Who doesn't?" The spring sky was a cheery sight to her weary eyes. There wouldn't be snow for the foreseeable future. *I hope, at least.* She was thoroughly finished with winter and the frigid temperatures.

Fifteen minutes later, she sat in a chair positioned perfectly to let the sun's rays wash over her. She'd stay there all day, sipping coffee and basking, if they'd let her.

"I miss talking to you."

Joci turned away from the large window and met Adrian's blue eyes. He was always direct. They both were. It worked some of their time together, but not always. Not today.

"What do you want me to say? That I do too?" She set down the ceramic cup and watched steam drift between them. "Because I do, but you destroyed our friendship and I'm wary to have the same kind again."

He took a bite of the blueberry muffin. "I know. Our issues are my fault. I take full responsibility. But I want to get back there again. Or something along those lines. Maybe even chat like we used to."

"Maybe one day." She shook her head. "But not yet. There's too much history."

He chuckled. "That's what you said last time…."

Joci swung her eyes to him. "Last time you didn't try to kill someone," she reminded him under her breath.

His face fell. "You're right. Sorry. I shouldn't have brought it up." He sipped his coffee and glanced around the bustling shop.

Wrapping her fingers around the cup, she stared at him. Adrian didn't deserve all of her wrath at any given moment, but he also hadn't earned any leniency either. It was a fine line she hadn't perfected.

"Are you planning on coming over this weekend to see Brett?"

Adrian pushed back from the table slightly. "I actually wanted to talk to you about that."

Joci narrowed her eyes. Already she didn't like the direction of the conversation.

"Can I have more than supervised visits? I understand—"

"No." She stood and gathered her purse. "I'm sorry, but no. I'm not ready for that, and neither are you."

"Joce, wait." He got to his feet and grabbed her arm. "Hear me out."

She scrunched her nose. "I don't have to, Adrian. Until I have answers about everything, you aren't taking my son anywhere unless I'm with him."

"He's my son too," he reminded her, tightening his grip.

Keeping her voice even, she jerked out of his reach. "Just because you're on the birth certificate doesn't mean you're his dad. He doesn't even have your last name. That shows you how certain I am that you'll fuck up. Again."

Adrian staggered back, pain scrawled on his features.

He held a hand over his sternum and winced.

She didn't wait for him to respond. His little act wasn't fazing her. He could fake a heart attack all he wanted, but it wouldn't change the truth of the matter. *He's fine. Just pretending.* Her feet faltered at the doorway. *Right?* She pushed her second-guessing aside. Adrian wasn't hers to worry about anymore.

Joci stepped out into the warming afternoon and headed toward the office. Adrian could handle the standing appointment with the judge. She had other clients to help.

***

Cameron rolled down the passenger window and took a deep breath. Spring was in the air once more. He couldn't wait to see what the warmer months would bring. *It can't get worse.* Scanning the neighborhood, he noted a few people waiting by the bus stop. None appeared to be doing anything illegal, so he kept searching. The convenience store nearby piqued his interest.

He looked over to see Quinn watching the radar gun, his green eyes anticipating the right combination of numbers so he could catch a speeder.

"I'm going to grab something to drink," Cameron said, opening the door. "Want anything?"

Quinn waved a hand. "Nah, I'm good, thanks."

Walking the short distance to the gas station, Cameron pulled open the door and nodded to the cashier before heading toward the refrigerated drinks. He scanned the wall filled with new and old favorites and opened one of the doors, deciding between flavors.

"And here I thought you didn't slack off when you were on duty."

Cameron gripped the cold energy drink as Bambi's voice hit him in the gut. "Stalking me now, huh?" He shut the door and glared at her. It wasn't unlike her to pop up where she wasn't wanted. In fact, it was one of her specialties. "Sounds like you."

Bambi flipped her blonde hair over her left shoulder. "You know I only stalk people I like." She offered him a haughty grin. "And you aren't in that realm anymore, Cameroni."

"Bummer," he said sarcastically and passed her.

"The next part of our job is ready."

This made him stop and turn around. He'd been impatiently waiting for those words—preferably from Jerry, not Bambi. "Want to fill me in so I can be done with you people?"

"You people?" She scoffed. "My family saved you. Jerry could've killed you years ago for your father's mishap. Not to mention the money you stole for me." She flicked his badge with her acrylic nail. Her touch all but caused his stomach to shrink in on itself. "You have him to thank for your fiancée and *bambino*. He orchestrated your defense, after all."

The police radio went off on his shoulder, and Cameron waited until the static ended to respond. "What's the plan? I need to get back to work."

"Meet us at the Ankeny airport tonight at seven."

She reached up and touched his wavy hair. "I miss this. It was always fun to mess up your hair." She pursed her lips and leaned closer. "We could start where we left off, you know. My brothers would probably give us a territory." She traced his lips, her blue eyes dark with lust. "Plus some."

Cameron grabbed her wrist and yanked it away from his mouth. "Fuck off. And while you're at it, leave Joci the hell alone."

"I do like a faithful man." Bambi chuckled darkly. "She truly doesn't deserve you."

"You're right. Joci deserves someone who doesn't bring a mob with him."

"And yet she stays. It must be love." She winked. "I'll see you tonight, Officer Shearer."

After blowing a kiss to the cashier, Bambi sashayed out of the convenience store. Cameron let out his breath and walked up to the counter.

"She a friend of yours?" the cashier asked with a broad grin.

Cameron pulled cash out of his pocket. "No, the opposite." He grabbed his change and left before the other man could say anything else. He didn't want to rehash any time spent with his devil of an ex.

Finding his partner in the same spot, he climbed into the SUV. "Did I miss anything?"

Quinn stopped typing on the laptop and looked toward the convenience store. "Nope. Did I?"

Opening the energy drink, Cameron took a long guzzle before answering. "Nothing to report here."

For a moment, Quinn squinted at him then returned to the computer. "You know you're a horrible liar, right?"

"What're you talking about? I'm a great liar."

"So nothing happened in the store just now?"

"Nada."

"Mm-hmm." Replacing the laptop to its spot, Quinn started the vehicle. "I don't know what bullshit you gave the captain about why you were fencing diamonds, but you aren't being truthful, and I'm not okay with it. Just like I'm not okay with that blonde chick all but following you everywhere we go."

Cameron's brow shot up. "What? She's following us?"

Quinn clipped his seat belt in place and shifted into gear. "For a mob guy turned cop, you don't check your six as much as I thought you would." He jerked a finger behind them. "Black Land Rover has been tailing us for the last week. I didn't want to say anything because I thought maybe they were the good mobsters. Judging from the look on your face after Bambi left the convenience store, I changed my mind."

"Shit." He looked over his shoulder. Sure enough, an SUV with dark tint followed a few cars behind. Just when he thought the mafia couldn't get more annoying. "She won't be any trouble. I'll talk to her." He sighed. "Again."

Quinn flicked on the blinker. "Not today, maybe. You can't keep lying, Cam. You aren't as good at it as you think. Joce sure as hell didn't buy your undercover cop story, and I doubt the captain did either." He glanced over. "We're all giving you a second chance; don't mess it up."

"I won't. Believe me, all I'm working on is getting myself out so I can be a cop and only a cop all the time." Cameron pulled out his phone and saw a missed call from Jerry. Sooner or later, he'd have to chat with Joci. The imminent danger was the only thing holding him back.

***

The clock on the wall of the therapist's office struck a new hour, and Joci waited for the appointment to start. Adrian hadn't showed up yet, a rare occurrence if the look on the receptionist's face meant anything. She checked her phone and frowned when no missed texts or calls from Adrian greeted her. She did have one from Cameron, though.

Cameron: Won't be able to make it tonight. Have to do some work stuff.

Joci: Okay. See you later then. Be safe.

She sighed. It was Del Rossi stuff, not law enforcement stuff. That much she gathered when he didn't answer. She'd get through the hour with Adrian and the therapist, then drown a few sorrows with Quinn and Rayna afterward.

Dr. Randall came out of his office after another five minutes. "Joci, why don't you come back?"

"Is Adrian here?" She reached the door to his office and peered inside, but no one sat on the couches.

"Um, no. He called a few minutes ago." Dr. Randall closed the door and motioned for her to sit. "He had a recent health scare, so he's at the hospital as a precaution. After his recent surgery, I understand his concern."

Joci's eyes bugged at the update. *Shit, was that thing in*

the coffee shop real? I'm a horrible person for leaving him alone. Her gut churned. "Oh, I'm sorry to hear that. I should leave and not waste your time then."

"Actually, I hoped to talk to you separately one of these times." He smiled. "Now seems as good as any, don't you think?"

"I suppose." She sank into the love seat and made herself comfortable. Well, as comfortable as she could get in a therapist's office.

"All right. So what's holding you back with Adrian?"

"Excuse me?"

"Well, he's mentioned that you're aloof, and you keep your son away as well."

She gripped the armrest. "You would be too if the man you once loved destroyed all of his relationships in one year. Did he tell you everything? The mob involvement? The gambling that led to being in debt with the mob? Or how about when the mob faked his death so they could use him as a pawn? Or maybe when he was part of a hit on Cameron's life?"

Dr. Randall sat quietly, pen unmoving. "Yes, he told me all that plus some. Adrian went through a lot, Joci."

"I understand, but it doesn't give him the right to waltz back into my life whenever it suits him." She smoothed her hands on her thighs. "Because that's what he does best. He'll come right when everything is going great and somehow mess it up."

"I believe you're referencing when the two of you attempted to reconcile."

She held up her hand. "I told him I'd try, not that we were. And that was only for the sake of the case."

"Cameron's case."

"Yes."

"Okay, what about when you fell for Cameron?" Dr. Randall tilted his head.

"I didn't mean to fall in love with him." She couldn't stop a smile from spreading over her cheeks. "It just happened. That's how love is supposed to be, right? Unexpected, out of the blue, and exactly what you need."

"So a mobster was what you needed?"

She chuckled. "No, definitely not, but I needed Cameron. Not because I was incomplete, but because when we're together I'm the best me. I can't say that about Adrian. I was the worst version of me when I was with him."

Dr. Randall jotted down a few notes. "And you believe if you let Adrian close again—to you or your son—something bad will happen?"

"Without a doubt."

"What do you think will happen?"

She shrugged. "I don't know. A mob kidnaps Brett or hauls Adrian off again."

"Can't that happen now? With Cameron?"

Joci's stomach dropped at the insinuation. Clearly, Adrian told the good doctor everything about their relationship. "Cam would never let anything like that happen."

Dr. Randall steered her toward another subject, but Joci zoned out. She could talk about her trust issues all night, but it wouldn't change her mind about Adrian.

Something didn't add up. Not with his appearance alongside Cameron's ex. They had to be connected. *But how?*

***

"And you're sure you want to do this?" Captain Valeria Eicher narrowed her dark eyes. "For real, this time. Not just a ploy to get out of prison time."

Cameron sank into the chair across from the captain and the FBI agent. He'd asked them to meet him after his mandatory court appearance that afternoon. Enough was enough when it came to Del Rossi. This was the best solution he could imagine.

Glancing around the now empty courtroom, he was grateful it'd been the last hearing of the day. Their subject wasn't one he wanted broadcast.

"Del Rossi needs to leave Iowa. If I can help, then I'm all for it."

Agent Stevens scratched his chin and reviewed the new information Cameron had given him. "The FBI can work with this."

"Does your fiancée know?" Valeria asked.

"No. Not yet. I'll tell her when it's the right time." He shook his head. "If this turns ugly, I want deniability for her and our family. They're my number-one priority. I brought the mob in, and I'll take them out."

"Brave of you," Stevens said, smirking. "Stupid, but brave." He stood. "All right, let me run this up the flagpole for legality sake."

"And my coercion with Del Rossi?"

"Covered with the immunity agreement." Stevens chuckled and waved the folder. "Which I assume one of your attorney friends helped you make."

"It helps to know people."

"I'll send over the final copy once legal has a look." Stevens nodded to Eicher, then walked out of the empty courtroom.

"The chief already gave me permission to do whatever's needed to get rid of Del Rossi. He doesn't care how, just that it's done." Valeria started toward the doors. "I'm glad you picked a side, Shearer. I was worried you wouldn't."

"I chose my family. No matter what happens to me, they need to be safe." He held her gaze until she understood the severity of his words. "Please, promise me that."

"I'll do everything in my power to keep Joci and the boys out of harm's way." She let out a small laugh. "But it won't be necessary, because you're going to be fine. Hell, you do this right and you'll be a hero."

Shaking his head, Cameron moved through the benches. "I don't want to be a hero. Just alive."

"Let's do both."

His phone rang, and he let out a shaky breath when he saw the name. "My immunity starts right away, doesn't it?"

Valeria glanced to his phone. "I'll expedite the paperwork with Stevens."

"I appreciate it."

"Big night planned?"

He chuckled and sent a reply. "You have no idea."

CHAPTER TWELVE

Cameron unbuttoned his police-issue coat when he arrived at the small airport a few miles north of Des Moines. He didn't want his law connection to be caught on film while he loitered with the Del Rossi mob. Whatever Jerry had planned needed to hurry up and be done already. His straight and narrow way of life was being disrupted too often for his liking.

He closed his Jeep door quietly and made his way to hangar thirteen. Italian words drifted on the wind, and he caught bits and pieces of conversations. He nodded to Jerry when he saw his boss next to a private airplane.

"What's the job?" He looked around and held in a disgusted glare when he spotted Bambi flirting with one of the pilots. She had no shame. Something that used to work well in their jobs.

Jerry clapped a bejeweled hand on the back of Cameron's shoulder and nodded to the white aircraft. "This plane once belonged to Mr. Ulrich."

"Am I supposed to know who that is?"

"Of course not. But you should." Jerry led him up the steps, and once they were seated in the cozy plane cabin, he continued. "Mr. Ulrich is a well-known stock market dealer. He owns a business in Chicago. One that owes me money, as it turns out."

"Then you're taking his plane until he repays the debt?"

"Yes and no." Jerry snapped his fingers and one of his bodyguards produced a beige envelope. "Ulrich was supposed to meet me this afternoon with a shipment of guns." His brows furrowed. "As it turns out, the man came early and sold my guns to the Mexican cartel."

Cameron shifted nervously on the leather seat. His boss didn't like being duped. If history had taught him anything, Jerry had more than a simple plan to get his guns and revenge.

"I don't like when people go back on their word." The mobster stared at Cameron. "Loyalty is equally as important as repaying debts."

"Agreed."

Jerry laced his chubby hands together. "Good, I'm glad you agree, because you and Bambi are going to rob this son of a bitch."

Cameron frowned. "Rob him? I thought he was based in Chicago."

"He is, but he also has a house here in the metro." He tossed Cameron the envelope. "In Des Moines, to be more exact."

Cameron eyed the envelope but didn't open it. "How does this tie in with Wong?"

"Nothing gets past you, does it?" Jerry laughed. "Wong and Ulrich are business partners."

"And they both wronged you," he put together and stood. The job was simple enough. They already had the diamonds from Mr. Wong and the cash thanks to the FBI allowing him to keep it for his undercover role. Now all he and Bambi needed to do was fleece Mr. Ulrich. A part of this didn't sit right in his stomach, though. "Why us?" He nodded to the two men who recently entered the plane. "Any of your thugs can pull this off."

Leaning forward, the chubby man smiled coldly. "Because I don't want them to do it. I want you and my baby sister. It means more, you see, if my favorites right an injustice done to me." He pulled out a small handgun from his waist and reviewed it. "Plus, it sends a message to anyone else who dares go back on their word." He cocked the gun but kept the barrel pointed to the floor. "Mr. Ulrich and Mr. Wong will be properly motivated to keep their side of our agreements going forward." He waved the gun. "Or I know of a bullet with each of their names on it."

Cameron nodded. He was fully aware Jerry wouldn't think twice before killing the businessmen. Naturally, the mob boss wouldn't pull the trigger. He'd get one of his henchmen to do the dirty deeds, like every other time. In all his years, he'd never seen the mafia boss kill anyone directly. Jerry's words were a silent warning too. No one walked away from the mob. He'd known since day one, and he was stupid enough to hope he was the exception. If Cameron didn't do everything demanded, his name might join the roster of bullets.

"When would you like us to complete this?"

"Tonight." Jerry looked behind him. "I believe my sister is ready to go."

Looking over his shoulder, Cameron held in a groan at the tight black outfit befitting a secret agent in a spy blockbuster. She was fully loaded with a gun on each hip and one in her hand. The plunging neckline of her shirt left very little to the imagination. He didn't know why she wore the damned thing. They were robbing a man, not seducing him. But that was Bambi.

I missed being there for Joci because of this. It was now obvious he'd also miss seeing his boys before bedtime too. Tonight was bound to be difficult in more than one way.

"All right, let's get going." He brushed by Bambi and felt a gun at the small of his back.

"Don't forget your weapon," she said cheekily, holding it up for him.

A million thoughts soared through his mind, but the need to live passed up his better judgment. He'd do this job. He had no choice.

Reaching the exit, he paused and looked to Jerry. "After this, I'm done." It was a statement, not a question. He'd more than fulfilled his duties.

The head of the Chicago mob simply nodded once.

Cameron sighed his relief but found it to be premature when Jerry said, "Good luck, Cameroni. Don't disappoint me. You know how it will end if you do."

He swallowed hard and disembarked the million-dollar

private plane. If no one died at the end of the night, he'd call it a good one. The hair stood on his arms, silently warning him to be cautious. Unfortunately, he wasn't sure which part of the evening would be the worst.

***

Aged scotch had never tasted so good as after the long hour spent with Adrian's therapist. Joci found a booth near the back of the bar and slid across the seat. Quinn would be there any minute, and she needed to settle her nerves before he arrived.

She took a sip and let out a breath, hoping to clear her mind of all things Adrian related. That lasted a whole thirty seconds. Dwelling on her conversation with Dr. Randall couldn't be helped. The more she found out about the time Adrian spent under Mikkelsen control, the more she pitied him. Enduring torture was one thing, but she'd never have imagined the daily struggle Adrian had to merely live.

With Adrian's consent, Dr. Randall had kindly given her the full medical file that Adrian brought when he returned to Des Moines. It included up-to-date records and even some therapy notes from his sessions.

Joci stared at the stack on the tabletop but couldn't bring herself to open them. She definitely didn't know why she'd brought them inside instead of leaving them in her car.

"Hey, Joce," Quinn greeted, breaking into her thoughts.

She looked up in time to see him sit and press a bottle of his favorite beer to his lips. He'd shed his police uniform and sported a casual pair of jeans and a red sweatshirt.

"Hey, thanks for coming early."

"No problem." He set down the beer on a coaster. "So what's up?"

Joci grabbed Adrian's records and set them on the seat next to her. They didn't need to dig into those yet.

"Well, we haven't hung out just the two of us in a while and I wanted to see how things were going." She grabbed the small menu. Her stomach had been growling since the moment she entered the place. Food was in order. "What's new with you?"

Quinn sat back and offered her a lazy smile. "Nothing, but you already knew that."

"I wouldn't go that far. I mean, my business partner seems to be very cheery lately." Joci lowered the menu and quirked her brow. "And humming a lot. Rayna isn't known for her singing abilities, Quinn, so I wonder what may have gotten into her." She paused and couldn't help but add, "Or who has gotten into her."

Choking on his gulp of beer, the off-duty cop sat up and pounded his chest with his fist. "Damn, way to be subtle, Joce."

She handed him a napkin. "Please, I've known you long enough to be anything but subtle."

He chuckled and wiped beer off his chin. "Yeah, I guess you're right."

The waitress arrived, and after Joci ordered a slew of appetizers, she continued her questioning.

"Are you screwing Rayna?"

A peculiar grin covered Quinn's face. Joci instantly

wanted to reach over and hug him. He was long over her, that much she could tell from the gleam in his green eyes.

"I don't think you really want to know the answer." He took another drink of beer and studied her. "Do you?"

"I wouldn't ask if I didn't," she countered, grateful to have a glass of water delivered. "But if you don't want to talk about it, I understand. Your private life isn't my business anymore. Honestly, it never really was."

Quinn laced his hands together on the table. "It's not that. We're friends, and even though we aren't as close as we used to be, I can't say anything. Rayna wouldn't appreciate it if I did. I think she's the one who wants to tell you." He paused. "If there's anything to tell."

Joci silently commended him. He wasn't normally tightlipped about anything with her. If he wasn't spilling details, it meant she'd cornered the wrong half of the couple.

"Good for you, Quinn." She held up her scotch. "I hope it works out." She smirked. "Whatever may or may not be going on with Rayna."

He clinked his bottle against her glass. "Yeah, yeah, now let's get down to the reason you wanted me to come early."

She sighed, suddenly not wanting to discuss Cameron. It was why she asked Quinn to come before Rayna, though.

"How's he doing? Be honest."

The waitress arrived with their appetizers, and Quinn started divvying up the tasty-smelling food. They'd end up ordering more once Rayna arrived, but for now, Joci was content simply sharing a meal with one of her closest friends.

He handed her a plate loaded with fries, chicken wings, fried pickles, and mozzarella sticks.

"I think he's struggling between Del Rossi and being a cop." He pointed a french fry at her. "And I'm pretty sure he's not being completely honest about his involvement."

Joci dipped a mozzarella stick in marinara sauce. "Yeah, I've known about that for a while."

"Why didn't you say anything?" He lowered his voice. "Look, I know I'm a cop, but I wouldn't rat him out to anyone unless he was hurting you or the boys."

She nodded and finished chewing. "That's just it. I would've told you, but I didn't want to incriminate you if things went haywire." She grabbed a napkin. "Ever since his ex-girlfriend came back into town, he's slipped further. Lying is one thing, but being caught by the Feds for a jewel exchange is a whole other thing. I don't know if I trust his double agent role. Seems too convenient given when he mentioned it."

Quinn finished off a chicken wing. "I was there when he first saw Bambi. I swear I've never seen anyone turn to ice like he did." He shook his head. "He was doing okay until she came around. That chick is bad news."

"I agree." She dipped a fried pickle in ranch dressing. "So, how're we going to steer him away from the dark side?"

He chuckled. "You and your *Star Wars* references. Gotta say, they never get old. It was one of the things I liked about you."

Joci rolled her eyes. "Rayna likes *Star Wars* too."

"True. Hmm, I wonder if she'd like roleplaying…." He coughed and stuffed a fry in his mouth before he could finish the thought. "Where is Cameron anyway? I thought he was meeting us here."

"He was." She looked to her phone and frowned at the lack of messages. "But something Del Rossi popped up, so he needed to take care of it."

Quinn's eyes narrowed. "Don't take this the wrong way, because I know how crazy you are for him, but are you really, honestly sure you want to be with him? Like forever?" He pointed to her engagement ring. "Because if you're not, it's okay. You saved his life more than once, and he's only brought mobsters to your doorstep. Everyone would understand if it was too much to deal with."

For a long moment, Joci ran his words over in her mind. Quinn was one of the best guys she'd ever met, and that didn't change even after she fell in love with another man.

"Thanks, Quinn, but I'm really, honestly sure." She smiled. "Cameron may be a little lost sometimes, but he's who I want and who I love. Mobster and all, he's it for me."

"Just had to check." He patted her hand and waved for another round despite the fact that Joci still nursed hers. "You're my friend, and your happiness matters, so if your mind ever changes, let me know and I'll help you in any way I can."

"My hero," she said dramatically.

"Ooh, Quinn's a hero now?" Rayna's cheerful voice interrupted.

Quinn slid over to let her sit next to him, but the redhead

chose the spot beside her partner. Joci couldn't help but notice his slight frown at Rayna's decision.

"Always been one, sweet cheeks," Quinn said before taking a gulp of beer.

Rayna's gray eyes flashed a mixture of embarrassment and desire before she slapped his hand away from the fries. "Nope, these are mine."

Quinn didn't seem put off, and in fact, he made it a point to graze his hand over Rayna's as they sparred back and forth about what food to order next. Joci sat back and watched the two. There was obviously something going on between them, and she wanted to know what. Seeing how Quinn's lips were sealed, she'd have to drag the details out of Rayna. It wouldn't be too difficult if Rayna drank one too many. The woman was anything but a vault when she drank.

For the next two hours, the three friends chatted, laughed, and ate until Joci swore they'd tried every appetizer on the menu. A rousing game of pool followed. Rayna won. She was a sneaky pool shark and wasn't afraid to flaunt it. It wasn't until after they played darts that Joci's phone rang.

She hustled over to their table and reviewed the restricted number on the caller ID. "Hello?"

"Joci Dorous?"

She covered her free ear with her hand to hear above the loud music and whoops from Quinn's recent victory. "Speaking."

"This is Sergeant Aikman from Polk County jail. We were told you are the attorney for Cameron Shearer. Is this correct?"

The words quickly sobered her and she gripped the phone tighter. "Yes."

"Great. Mr. Shearer is currently being held on bail for robbery in the first degree."

The recently digested food in her stomach threatened to come back up. "What?" she whispered, and her legs started to shake.

"He was caught in a Des Moines residence without authorization and had a handgun."

She closed her eyes, and a tear slipped down her cheek. "Okay, I'll be there shortly." She hung up and sank into the seat, gut rolling.

"Hey, Joce, you okay? You look really white." Rayna came over and leaned on the table. "Like Adrian Petosa white."

"No, I'm not okay."

Quinn quickly assessed the scene, and his smile dropped. After he met her eyes, he cursed loudly. "What'd he do?"

She couldn't stop the tears after that. She fell in love with a bad boy; asking him to be anything else was pointless.

CHAPTER THIRTEEN

The thin mattress did little to hide the hard frame beneath it. Cameron stared at the ceiling and recalled the last time he was in this exact cell. Tonight was different. He wasn't pumped full of drugs and drowsy. The cops had caught him red-handed, and he more than earned the disgruntled exchange between jailers when they moved him to the secluded cell. He couldn't give away his double role, even if it'd help. Del Rossi had men in the jail staff. He'd heard Jerry discussing it in passing. Chancing anything before the FBI and police scheme started wasn't in the cards.

Rolling to his side, he watched the shuffle of feet near the door. If he had to guess, someone was mopping the floors. He tenderly rubbed his jaw. It hurt something fierce, thanks to being smacked by Bambi. It was supposedly an accident when they entered the ritzy mansion. Judging from how hard she hit him, Cameron couldn't write it off as happenstance. It didn't matter. They'd had a job to do.

They managed to steal all the items Jerry listed to let Mr. Ulrich know he wasn't beyond Del Rossi reach. As it turned out, they'd tripped a silent alarm, and the police arrived before they could both escape. Bambi saw them arrest him. He'd seen her nose sticking out of the nearby bushes. By now, her brother knew, and it was only a matter of time before he was out on bail. *I hope.*

He'd kept his mouth shut about his coconspirator. Del Rossi demanded as much. He never snitched, and he was already up to his neck playing both sides. He couldn't give away Bambi. Not when they needed the whole mob.

The embarrassing part happened when Eicher, Stevens, and the police chief himself came down when Cameron arrived. The chief promptly took away Cameron's service weapon and badge, putting him on unpaid leave while a thorough investigation ensued. Even though the chief knew about his undercover role, he wanted to make a statement in case Del Rossi was watching. If they simply released him, the mob would be suspicious. His cover was successfully maintained for the time being. *Sure hope it stays that way.*

That was shit he could handle on his own. What he wasn't so sure about was the part where the jail called Joci after they booked him. It was bound to happen. She was his fiancée and attorney, but he'd hoped they'd wait until morning.

Now, three hours later, Cameron watched a fly land on the floor as the minutes ticked by quietly. He hoped Joci didn't answer and was fast asleep with their boys in the next room. Knowing she'd been out with Quinn and Rayna, he doubted that was the case.

His gaze slid to the green jumpsuit covering his

tattooed body. It wasn't his favorite apparel. He stood and paced the small area, frustrated with himself more than anything. *I should've checked the specs before we entered the house.* He shook his head. He'd been out of the game too long. Technology had improved tenfold since the last time he ran a heist. *Fuck, I'm slipping.*

Voices bounced down the hallway, and he gripped the metal bars and closed his eyes. One was familiar. *Very familiar.* He looked up and saw the jailer unlock the door and slide it open. Beside him stood Joci. Her face was masked in the same emotion she used in court.

Notwithstanding her stiff façade, she looked gorgeous. Her hair was pulled back into a braid, and her jeans and turquoise long-sleeved blouse were fashionable and delectable on her. She wouldn't look him in the eye. That part cut him deep. He didn't deserve to be graced with her gaze, but he yearned for it.

"Thanks, Larry," she said once the older man walked in the opposite direction. Only then did she look up long enough to say, "Let's go."

Cameron hurried through the open door and caught up with her. "Joce, look, I—"

"Do not say another word until we're out of here," she fumed, picking up her pace.

He nodded and followed her through the doors. Once they gathered his belongings, they walked out to the parking lot, lit up with tall lights. It was impossible to escape the jail and not be seen. There was enough light to illuminate the entire area plus some.

Joci paused beside her car and turned to face him. "How could you do this, Cam?"

Her hazel eyes flashed ire, and he held up his hands. "I wasn't supposed to get caught."

Her hands rested on her hips. "Really, you don't say?" The sarcasm on her lips never sounded worse. Normally, he loved it, but not tonight.

Walking over, he placed his hands over hers. "I'm sorry. The job didn't go as planned. Bambi got away, but I didn't." He frowned. "Honestly, that might have been what Jerry planned."

"Why would he want you arrested? You're more valuable out of jail."

"I don't know." He rubbed his hands up her arms, but she backed away. "But I'll find out. If Jerry did it on purpose, he'll own it."

Joci rubbed her eyes and let out a frustrated grunt before climbing into the driver seat. The car lurched forward before he could shut his own door.

They traveled in complete silence. Not even the radio hummed in the background. Cameron chanced a glance to Joci every few minutes, but she remained focused on traffic. Her jaw was clenched tightly, and when she pushed her glasses up her nose, he sighed loudly.

"Joce, come on, talk to me. Yell at me. Scream. Cry. Whatever. I don't care. Just talk to me," he begged. "Please."

She slowed for a red light and glared at him. "I don't even know what to say. When you said, 'One more job,' I thought it wouldn't include jail time. Some danger, sure, but actually being caught by the authorities not once but twice?" She glanced back to the traffic light. "That didn't cross my mind."

"Me either." He rubbed the back of his neck. "My guess is Jerry doesn't want me to leave. If I get fired from my job and have no one to turn to except him, he wins."

She took a corner a little too fast, and he gripped the console. "He better not think that or he'll have another thing coming."

Cameron held in a chuckle. A look of absolute murder was scrawled on her pretty face. She couldn't do a damn thing and would never hurt anyone, but it was endearing to know she'd always be in his corner to help.

"I'll sort it all out with Jerry tomorrow. Bambi got away with the shit he wanted, so he'll make this case disappear like all the others." He rested his head on the headrest and closed his eyes.

"You honestly think it's that simple?"

"Yep. Jerry will handle it."

She let out a disbelieving laugh. "Right, because he's such a gem."

"Jerry may be a lot of things, but he'd never abandon me." He looked over and heard her curse under her breath. Even he didn't believe the words. Relying on Del Rossi was foolish, if the last ten years taught him anything.

Fifteen minutes later, the car pulled into their garage, and she didn't wait for him before walking into the house. Cameron followed at a slower pace, pushing the button to close the garage door. He'd thought for certain that she'd ship him off to Quinn's or even make him sleep in the jail cell for the night. *This is worse.*

The late hour shone on the microwave clock. He heard the nanny leave through the front door as he slipped off his shoes. Walking into the living room, he saw Joci toss a blanket and pillow on the couch.

"Joce—"

"Nope." She waved her index finger at him. "You want to act like a dumbass, then you get to sleep on the couch like one."

He opened his mouth to argue, but the expression on her face clamped his lips shut again. Nodding, he resigned himself to the fact that the couch would be his punishment for the foreseeable future.

Joci whipped through the room, picking up discarded baby toys. She liked to clean when she was upset, and from the way she grabbed the small train from the table, he gathered she was livid.

"I'll clean up," he offered, prying the toys from her.

She ignored him and kept up her flurry until the living room was pristine. Pausing at the hallway, she looked over her shoulder. "Don't make me regret bailing you out."

That's a common theme lately. Cameron identified the pain in her eyes. He'd put it there, and that knowledge hurt worse than being exiled to the couch. "I won't." She let out a breath, then padded down the hallway. The resounding click of the master bedroom door lock made him plop onto the couch face-first. Major damage control was in order for the following day. For now, he'd try to sleep without Joci's fuzzy bun poking his face. Somehow, he missed it.

***

Joci woke the next morning spooning the pillow beside her. She frowned and punched it lightly. This wasn't how she preferred to wake up. *Cameron's lips on my neck would be much better.* Shivering, she noticed the comforter at the end of the bed. Cameron usually kept her nice and toasty when she kicked off the blankets. Evidently, her mind didn't remember how she'd tossed her heater to the couch.

Replacing his pillow to its spot, Joci sat up and stretched. Her neck ached, but she wasn't sure if she could blame it on Cameron or the cases she'd read before falling asleep. Either way, a massage was suddenly a priority.

She grabbed her phone from the bedside table and noticed messages from Quinn, Rayna, and even Adrian. All were checking on how she was feeling after Cameron's arrest. Pushing them off until later, she pulled on a pair of warm socks and opened the bedroom door.

Childish laughter filled the air, and from the sound of it, they were in the kitchen. Joci double checked the twins' room and smirked when she saw it tidy. Cameron's ass kissing had already begun.

She walked into the kitchen in time to see Brett spit out his blue baby food. She chuckled when some of it hit Cameron's cheek. The baby giggled at the disgusted look on his face, causing him to do it all over again with the next spoonful. Cameron egged on the behavior each time Brett spit it back at him.

Joci leaned against the counter and grinned when Levi decided to try the same game. It was touching how good Cameron was with their boys. He hadn't missed one thing in their short lives, and she knew he never would. Despite not having a great role model, Cameron was an exceptional dad.

Finding a mug, she filled it with coffee and watched them over the rim. By the time the boys finished breakfast, Cameron was covered in what smelled like mashed blueberries. A little even dribbled down his shirtless torso. Standing, he offered her a smile before rinsing off the dishes and himself, then pulled on a fresh shirt from the dryer.

"I didn't know breakfast was so funny," she commented, watching the twins smear leftovers on their trays.

Cameron grabbed a wet wipe and headed toward the boys. "I guess to these little guys, it is." He finished cleaning them up and set them in their saucer activity centers. They didn't seem to mind being apart while they teethed on the toys.

He came back to the kitchen and sat on one of the barstools across from her. "So how long will my banishment to the couch be?"

Joci sipped on her coffee, not wanting to answer because she didn't have one yet.

"If it's a while, I think I'll stop by the store and buy a blow-up mattress." He massaged his left shoulder. "The couch was definitely made for sitting, not sleeping."

In her own way, she felt his pain. Not having him beside her last night wasn't something she wanted to repeat if she could help it. Still, he needed to talk to her. Explain his behavior.

"I guess it'll depend on what other trouble you get into before it's time for bed again," she replied, looking at the clock. She had about an hour before her appointment at the office. If she hurried, she'd shower and get there in time.

Before she could escape the conversation, Cameron stood and wrapped his arms around her waist. His brown eyes searched for hers, and once he caught them, she swallowed hard. Repentance lined the depths, and in her heart, Joci realized she'd forgiven him the moment she saw him in the jail cell. It reminded her too much of when they reconnected. He wasn't the same thug as back then. He'd changed, and so had she.

"I can't begin to say how sorry I am, babe." He cupped the back of her neck, guaranteeing her undivided attention. "I wasn't thinking about the consequences. I was only dreaming about getting the job done so I was finished with Del Rossi. It was a mistake no matter how I look at it. If I could go back and change what happened, I would."

Joci bit her bottom lip. The unshed tears in his eyes weren't manufactured. She doubted he could ever be that manipulative. Reaching up, she traced his jaw that held more than a day's growth. It pricked her fingers, but she didn't care. She loved every rough edge of this man.

"I forgive you." The tension in his shoulders seemed to evaporate, and she hugged him close. "I didn't like seeing you back there, Cam. It's not where you belong. Not anymore."

Cameron gently captured her lips beneath his. She clung to the front of his shirt. She'd never tire of him. No matter how many years passed, he'd always have her heart and every ounce of her desire.

He pulled back and kissed the side of her neck. "I don't fucking deserve you, Joci."

She smirked and grabbed his face, kissing him hard. "Yes, you do."

"I don't, but I love that you think I do." He lifted her to the counter and settled between her thighs. "When are you marrying me again?"

"Soon."

"Not soon enough." He traced her earlobe with his tongue. "I want everyone to know you're mine."

Joci's heart swelled at his words. "I'm always yours."

Wrapping her legs around his waist, she plunged her fingers through his wild hair. She'd stay there all day if her schedule allowed it. Losing Cameron wasn't an option. She was in for the long haul, whether it broke her heart or not.

CHAPTER FOURTEEN

"You have to do this, Joci. You can't keep putting it off."

She stared at the stack of Adrian's medical records. They'd been on the edge of her desk for two weeks. The one time she attempted to read them, she chickened out at the last second. It was all so personal and invasive.

Grabbing the first file, she took a deep breath. "I can do this." She recognized it as the hospital records directly after leaving Iowa. The CAT scans, MRI results, and blood tests didn't look abnormal. *Then again, you have no idea what you're looking at.*

She huffed and flipped through the pages. From the doctor notes to nurse summaries, it all concluded what the neurologist explained to her after Adrian's surgery. Something bad happened to him, and not just the car bomb.

Photos of his skin transplants from surgery to recovery made her stomach queasy, but she was used to homicide snapshots. She could handle this. Swallowing hard at the picture of the scar on Adrian's face, she shook her head. *Maybe I can't.*

She closed her eyes and took a moment to center her thoughts. Reviewing these files as a friend or family member was the wrong approach. Staying indifferent was the only way she'd finish before meeting with Adrian and his therapist again.

Three hours later, Joci slouched in her chair and rubbed her temples. Information overload was putting it lightly. Someone needed to translate the medical jargon or she'd go insane with the research ahead of her.

Recalling Tad O'Brien, the paramedic who seemed to be everywhere, she dialed the main number for Mercy hospital, and the receptionist gave his station information.

"I'm following up on a lead," she called, walking out of her office.

"Okay, if your lead goes by any smoothie place, call me," Rayna shouted back. "I'd sell my soul for something chocolatey with peanut butter."

Joci chuckled and made a mental note to stop by such a place on her way back to the office. Twenty minutes later, she sat in a fire station waiting area. Tad was on his way back from a hospital drop off and would be back shortly.

Fifteen minutes later, his familiar voice greeted her. "Joci Dorous, attorney extraordinaire. I never imagined I'd see you here."

She stood. "And I never thought I'd be here either, though I'm not sure about that last part."

Tad waved her back toward the offices. "Your cop fiancé seems to think so." He guided her to a small room with a desk and three chairs. "Now, what can I do for you?" he asked, sitting behind the desk.

Joci glanced around the office. Other than an inspiration poster of a golf course, it was bare. With his job, he didn't spend much time there anyway.

"I wanted to see if you could help me make sense of these records." She lifted the stack. The therapy notes weren't difficult to understand. It was the medical ones she needed assistance with. "I already spoke to a neurologist, but I want someone who will give it to me straight. From what I've gathered, you're the man for the job."

"There's a good chance, yeah." He sat back and propped his legs on the desk. "And who exactly do these belong to?"

"My ex-husband."

Tad's brows rose. "Is that so?"

"He gave them to me," she rushed to say. "I didn't steal them. He's trying to be forthright in his medical past, and some of the terminology is lost on me."

Taking the offered files, Tad scanned the first one. "Are you sure you want to know?"

"If I can understand more about what he went through, I think we can try a friendship again."

"Sure." For a minute, he read the pages, flipping through them quietly. "It looks pretty cut-and-dried to be honest. No crazy tests or results." He cleared his throat. "I'm still on shift. Can you give me a few days to review these?"

"Oh yeah, sorry. Take all the time you need." She stood and moved for the door.

"Do you honestly think this information will change your perception of Adrian?"

Turning, Joci bit her bottom lip. "I'm not sure. On one hand, he was a pawn and used by an awful man. On the other, it doesn't add up. I like my facts black and white. It's how I do my job. With Adrian, everything is a shade of gray."

Chuckling, Tad thrummed his fingers on the edge of the desk. "Yeah, medical shit isn't the same. Don't get me wrong, there's plenty of black and white, but there's a ton more we can't understand." He pointed to a test result. "Like this. Adrian's blood test results show he was exposed to high levels of lead. That could mean he spent a lot of time in a condemned building."

"Which would align with his statement about being held against his will somewhere sketchy in Mexico."

He turned to another page. "And here, they mention skin grafts that appear to have been contaminated before use." He shrugged. "The possibilities are endless, Joci. You can read these until you're blue in the face and still not know what Adrian went through." He pushed the files toward her. "I don't think I can help you. Not in the way you want."

"What do you mean?"

"I can't make your decision about Adrian. No one can except you." He yawned and glanced at the watch on his right wrist. "I'm happy to translate specific things, but that's it."

His reasoning suddenly made sense. She didn't necessarily need to know every detail of Adrian's medical history. It was subjective, since Adrian couldn't remember all the details of his time with the Mikkelsen mob.

Slightly disappointed, Joci retrieved the stack. "Yeah, you're right. I was afraid of that. Damn you for being smart."

He grinned. "Careful, your fiancé will kick my ass if he hears you've been complimenting me."

She rolled her eyes. "Not what I meant, O'Brien. But thank you anyway. I needed a little common-sense reminder."

"Happy to help. Now, if you'll excuse me, I'm going to catch a few winks before my next call." He opened the office door at the same time dispatch came over the loudspeaker. "Or not." He hustled down the hallway. "You can see yourself out, right?"

"Definitely. Go save lives."

He waved, then disappeared around a corner. Alone again, Joci stared at the medical records in her hands. She'd been over them twice. None mentioned deceit or an evil plot to take over the world. Not that she'd been looking for the latter. *Probably.*

Trudging to her car, she nestled the files on the passenger seat. She had answers, both physical and mental. The emotional ones were her only hang-up.

***

The methodical sound of typing kept Cameron company in the small waiting area. He'd dropped off the twins to Joci an hour ago in order to meet with the FBI. She thought he was going to the station to deal with his recent suspension.

Little does she know.

He ran a hand through his hair, the longer length flopping

over his brows. Normally, it was gelled during shifts. Cutting it short again wasn't what he wanted. It was inevitable in his line of work, but until his commanding officer told him to trim it, he'd leave it alone as long as possible.

The strong scent of freshly brewed coffee reminded him of Joci. She'd looked stunning as usual this morning in black leggings and an oversized yet stylish off-the-shoulder sweater. Thankfully, her schedule was light, just a phone conference before he dropped off the boys so she could watch them while he was away.

"Shearer, we're ready for you," Agent Stevens said from the doorway.

Patting his thighs once, he stood and followed the FBI agent down the hallway and into an office.

"So, anything new to report?" Stevens asked, sitting behind the desk and clicking on his keyboard.

"Jerry's keeping everything close," Cameron started. "I'm a little surprised. He knows I want out, but he's never been one to keep his mouth shut." He smirked. "In fact, Jerry likes to blab a lot."

Stevens's brow furrowed. "Then he's onto you."

"I thought that too, but when I met him last night, he acted like nothing had changed." Cameron thought back to the short chat he and Jerry had had at the bakery up the road from the courthouse. The irony wasn't lost on him either. Jerry chose the location for a reason. Mostly to remind Cameron that he was above the law. *For now.*

"Well, he wouldn't. Not yet." Stevens slid a stack of papers to him. "Legal tweaked your agreement a smidgen, but nothing major. Review and sign, and you're good to go." He chuckled. "You're officially an undercover officer for DMPD and a CI for the FBI. Congrats."

Cameron scanned the document, sheet by sheet. It looked similar to the one he'd put together. Altogether, it covered his ass for past, present, and future mafia crimes. He couldn't go wrong with this kind of deal. Prison wasn't an option ever but especially these days. Unless Del Rossi killed him, Cameron wasn't going anywhere.

"Looks good." He scribbled his signature on the last page.

Agent Stevens signed as well, then made a copy. "The tech guys will need a little of your time before you leave." He stood and shook Cameron's hand. "We're going to get these sons of bitches for good."

Cameron tucked his copy of the immunity agreement in his back pocket. "I'm counting on it."

***

Popping the last pretzel bite in her mouth, Joci frowned. Her thighs didn't need the extra carbs, but soft pretzels were too tempting to resist. Especially since they were right next to the indoor playground at the mall. She'd earned a little guilty pleasure after the week she'd had. Too many court hearings had gone awry, and only carbs could make it better.

"Keep eating those and you'll never fit into your wedding dress," Rayna teased from the small slide where she held Brett at the top.

Joci gave her a sassy glare and tossed the empty bag in

the trash. She carefully stepped around other children until she reached her dynamic duo. They were moving about the spongy flooring as quickly as their chubby legs allowed. Rayna was down on the floor with them, her auburn hair pulled back in a bun on top of her head. With no makeup and a sparkling smile, any woman would be jealous.

"Good thing I haven't purchased a dress then, huh?"

Rayna shrugged and settled on her knees. "Speaking of, when are you two getting married? I mean, not to rush you or anything. I know you're not exactly sprinting down the aisle."

Finding a bench near the crawling boys, the two sat and watched the children play. Out of the ten in the playground, Brett and Levi were the youngest. Naturally, that meant all the youngsters had to check out the cuties. She didn't mind. It was nice to have the attention on them.

"Cam and I are waiting for the right time." She took off her glasses and cleaned the lenses. "So far, our timing has been sucky."

"Because of the mob?"

"Partly, yeah." She saw Brett lift himself on his little legs and scan the area for her. Once he spotted her, a wide grin covered his face and he turned toward her. "Adrian has a little to do with it, only because of his disappearing then reappearing act."

"I understand that. Adrian is a wild card. Hell, he might even object."

"He wouldn't be invited, Ray."

"Girl, please. You've seen enough romance movies to

know that doesn't stop men."

Thinking it over, Joci crossed her legs. "True, but Adrian knows there's nothing between us."

"Nothing but a child." Rayna giggled when Levi started crawling toward the exit. After corralling him back to his brother, she sat on the floor beside the bench. "This kid acts so much like Cameron. Already trying to escape his confines."

Her words gave Joci pause. Was that how everyone saw Cameron? As a person trying to get away? Frowning, she pulled her phone from her purse and reviewed the missed text messages.

Adrian: I'm on my way. Please don't leave.

From the time stamped on the message sent, he'd be there soon. She scrolled to the next one.

Quinn: Hey, can you remind Rayna to come early before court tomorrow? I need to discuss the case.

That one made Joci hold in a laugh. She gave Rayna a sideways glance. Her partner knew her court schedule better than any other attorney she'd met.

Joci: Or you could tell her yourself.

Her best friends were hilarious in a frustrating way. *I better be a whole city away when they finally announce they're dating.*

"Are you going to take his last name?"

Glancing up, she lifted her brows. "That came out of nowhere."

Rayna chuckled. "I just thought of it." She gently tickled Levi. "You never took Adrian's name."

"No."

"Why not?"

She pursed her lips. "Maybe somewhere in the back of my mind, I knew we wouldn't be forever."

"Mm-hmm, and what about Cameron?" Rayna asked, tilting her head to the side. "Is he your forever?"

A rush of memories involving Cameron invaded her, causing a smile to line her lips. "Yeah, he's my forever."

Rayna beamed. "Then I guess I'll start calling you Mrs. Shearer."

Before she could respond, Adrian's voice cut in.

"Good, you didn't leave."

Seeing Adrian heading their direction, Rayna went back to playing with the twins.

"Hey, yeah, the boys love this place."

He slipped off his shoes and carefully folded his suit jacket before plopping down next to the twins. Brett immediately recognized him, and a loud squeal set him off toward his dad.

"Where's Cameron?" Adrian asked, coaxing Brett closer.

"Being a badass," Rayna said, hopping onto the bench.

Adrian's light brows lifted. "What?"

"He's finishing up some things at the station," Joci filled in, retrieving Levi before he tumbled. She propped him on her knee. "Police stuff."

"Like I said, badass." Standing, Rayna grabbed her purse. "I need to head out. Thanks for the pretzel, Joce." She leaned down and said goodbye to the twins before walking into the throng of the mall.

"I see she still thinks I'm the devil." Adrian zoomed Brett like an airplane. "Think that'll ever change?"

Levi grabbed a handful of her hair and yanked. "It's possible." She gave Levi a toy to squeeze instead. "Do you honestly care what she thinks?"

Sitting up, Adrian wiped a string of drool from his hand. "Not really. But Rayna is your best friend. No matter what happens, she'll always be around, so I'd prefer she doesn't hate me."

Joci perused the playground and finally settled on Adrian. He couldn't look more out of place if he tried. Without a doubt, he was the best-dressed person in the mall. That hadn't changed. *It never will.* Since the moment she met him, he'd loved being fashionable.

She rubbed her lips together and watched him play with Brett. Little by little, she was letting herself trust him. He practically begged to do things with Brett, since he'd already missed so much. So long as she was there, Adrian could tag along. That had been a contentious subject with Cameron. *It still is.* But they'd agreed to give Adrian a little rope and see what he did with it.

"I went through your medical files." She set Levi on the floor when he started wriggling. "And the therapy notes."

"Okay?"

"And I believe you, Adrian."

He kept his gaze focused on Brett, but a content smile crossed his face. "Thanks, Joce." His blue eyes collided with hers. "You don't know how much that heals me."

She moved beside him and stole the drooling baby. "We

can't be the same as we once were."

"Yeah, I know." He grinned at Levi when he started crawling on his leg. "I'll take what I can get. Just spending time with my son is better than I could imagine."

"Are you sure? Because you—"

"No." Adrian swiveled his torso and scanned her face. "What I truly want will never happen. But eventually, I'll move past it." He offered her a weak smile. "I can't just stop loving you, Joci. It's not a switch I can turn off."

"Sure, I understand." She didn't. Not entirely, but she'd pretend for his sake.

"All right, now that we have that settled, how do you feel about weekly family dinners?"

Adrian tucked Levi under one arm and Brett under the other, then stood and slowly spun them in a circle. Both boys giggled loudly. After a few rotations, he plopped beside her. "Wow, I should not have done that after eating tacos."

"Weekly family dinners sound great to start." She smiled and held her emotions in check when she noticed the misting tears in his eyes. He cleared his throat and looked away, but she'd seen them. She'd learned enough about the gaps in Adrian's time away. They could focus on the future as friends.

Getting everyone else on board with it would be another mountain. *For another day.*

CHAPTER FIFTEEN

A week flew by while Cameron stayed home with the twins. The nanny came to help around the house, but he was on his own for the most part. It would've been fine had he not been called to the police department to discuss his undercover assignment. His meetings with the FBI investigators were laborious and not something he ever wanted to do again. Being a CI was exhausting.

Jerry managed to sneak under the skin of one of the county attorneys enough for the charges to be lessened, though not dropped entirely. It wouldn't happen until the FBI allowed it anyhow. Once his mission was complete, the FBI would wipe the case away. He wasn't worried, but Joci was extremely stressed, and he didn't like that.

Cameron put away the last bit of silverware from the dishwasher. His fiancée was on edge, and he couldn't blame her. While she eventually let him sleep in their bed again, her behavior was more elusive than ever. He needed to tell her about his partnership with Captain Eicher and the FBI to reel in Del Rossi. Part of him wouldn't allow it. Keeping her safe—their boys safe—was his goal. Deniability was his best option in case things went sideways with Del Rossi.

His phone chirped a new message.

Jerry: The men contacted me. Get over here.

He sent a reply saying he was on his way. After a quick change and kiss to both boys, he left them with their nanny and headed toward Jerry's hotel. None of this sat right in his gut.

He gripped the steering wheel a little tighter and watched the drizzle on the windshield. Del Rossi was always a gamble, but with Bambi in town, the mob suddenly became toxic for his life. He felt the downward spiral even if he couldn't see it. Telling himself it was the last job didn't feel right. He'd never heard of anyone getting out of the mafia unless it was in a body bag.

Easing the Jeep into the parking lot, he drove around the back and parked in an open spot. He sent a text message to Joci and stared at the screen. She was in depositions all day with Adrian; she'd said so before leaving that morning. A little part of Cameron was jealous of the time they spent together. He trusted her with his life, but Adrian was a different beast entirely.

He sent another text to Captain Eicher, then one to Agent Stevens. They'd both kept close tabs on him since his release from jail. His goal was to disband Del Rossi or try to get enough information for someone else to do it. Between the two agencies, he'd get it done.

Cameron stepped out of the Jeep and nodded at one of Jerry's security guys before entering the lavish hotel.

The business mogul had bought a string of hotels so he had a nice place to stay whenever he visited Des Moines. Over the last few months, his visits became longer and more frequent. A fact Cameron wasn't fond of in the least. Bambi was the reason, if he had to guess.

Winding down the hallways, he found his benefactor sitting in a large leather chair, smoking a cigar. Jerry's salt-and-pepper hair was slicked back, and his designer three-piece suit reminded Cameron that the man had money to burn. With smooth jazz in the background and a cognac in his other hand, Jerry couldn't look more old-school mobster if he tried.

"Ah, there you are." Jerry sat up enough to put his glass on a nearby table. His dark eyes glistened with something devious, and Cameron wasn't sure he wanted to stay long.

"Did the county attorney drop my case yet?" He glanced over to the wet bar and saw Bambi make a martini. "Since you wanted me to get caught and not Bambi."

Jerry put a hand to his heart as if the words hurt him. "Now, Cameroni, you know I'd never do anything to put your life in jeopardy."

Cameron shoved his hands in the front pockets of his jeans. "Yeah, of course not."

Snickering, the mob boss puffed his cigar. "But, no, the county attorney is holding strong to your case. Something about a cop not being above the law." He smirked. "Too bad Adrian can't get you out of this jam, eh?"

"I wouldn't want to owe him anything."

Bambi giggled in the background. Her heeled shoes

echoed on the flooring and her perfume filled the space when she walked closer. She took a sip of her martini with three green olives and patted Cameron's arm. He instantly recoiled, not wanting any part of her touching him. She was a disease.

"Adrian and Joci really are a cute couple," Bambi cooed, walking around him, hand grazing his back.

"So were we once upon a time," Cameron said between clenched teeth. "That doesn't mean you're supposed to be with someone."

Bambi pouted and downed the rest of her drink. She tossed the empty glass behind her, and it shattered on impact. Inching closer, she traced his face with her fake nails.

"Too bad. Ever since my return, I've found I miss you." Her hand dipped down his chest and rested on his belt. "Especially certain parts of you."

Cameron looked to Jerry. The older man merely sniggered and studied his cigar. "Back off, Bambi. You're the reason I'm in this mess." He tried to escape her grip, but she'd linked her fingers beneath the belt. If he touched Bambi roughly, he was as good as dead. They all knew it too. The bodyguards in the room would jump him within seconds.

She let out a bark of laughter and glanced to Jerry. "Tell me, brother, would you let Cameron out of Del Rossi if he slept with me one more time?"

Sucking in a hiss, Cameron swore his jaw would break with how tight he held it. The potential answer paralyzed his lips.

Jerry shrugged. "Sure, why not? If it makes my sister happy, I have no objection." He raised his drink in salute. "What do you say, Shearer?"

"I'd rather jump into a meat grinder," he replied without missing a beat.

Bambi leaned up and kissed him soundly. He jerked back and wiped off the red lipstick smeared on his lips.

"What the hell?" He glared at her, then Jerry. "Why am I here? You asked me to come, and it better not have been to humiliate me."

The mob boss sobered and squinted. "Why? What would you do if that was my plan?"

Adrenaline coursed through Cameron's veins. He took a step backward. "Jerry, don't fuck with me. I've been loyal to Del Rossi. All I want is out. You gave me your word—"

"And what kind of boss would I be if I didn't jerk you around a bit?" He shooed Bambi away and stood. "You have been loyal to the mob, Cameroni, but I don't want to lose assets either. You and Joci are great ones to utilize."

Cameron ran his fingers through his hair, not giving a damn how messy it looked now. "I can't, don't you understand? I chose another life. I can't go back to this."

Jerry reached him and put both hands on Cameron's shoulders. Looking him straight in the eye, he said, "Finish the job and you're free." Cameron almost gave the man a hug until he added, "But you'll be on my payroll part-time until I say so."

He parted his lips to argue, but Jerry gripped Cameron's chin. "That isn't a request, Shearer. It's all I can offer without being seen as soft."

Swallowing hard, he accepted the words. The alternative wasn't one he wanted. He was rather fond of breathing.

"You never truly leave the mob, you just learn to live with it," Jerry finished, then gave him a kiss on each cheek. "Now, as to the reason I asked you here." He sat back in his chair. "Ulrich and Wong made contact. They want to make peace and pay their debts. You and Bambi will collect their payment and ensure we no longer have to deal with them."

Cameron looked over to see Bambi cocking a gun. He closed his eyes for a moment, then opened them. His gaze landed on a large man walking into the room. He'd only met the bulky guy once, and that one time was enough to ingrain the cleaner for Del Rossi in his mind. Every good mob had one. The man who loomed a good four inches above Cameron was more than that, though. He was also Del Rossi's assassin and an excellent one at that.

"You've met Charlie Gambino, yes?" Jerry asked, lighting a new cigar.

He nodded and hoped Jerry didn't further investigate. He momentarily met Charlie's eyes. Their history wasn't one either wanted to discuss, especially in front of their mob boss.

"Good. Charlie will ensure the job is done correctly," Jerry continued with a cold smile. "And if not, he'll properly dispose of the problem."

The dark promise was more than evident. If Cameron stepped out of line and didn't get rid of Ulrich and Wong, Del Rossi would get rid of him.

"We'll take care of it," he said, motioning for Bambi to follow him. To his dismay, Charlie brought up the rear of their little death mob. Suddenly, being in the Polk County jail sounded like a much better way to spend his day.

***

Knocking softly on the wood door, Joci waited until she heard Adrian's voice bid her entrance to open it. She straightened her shoulders and walked in with her head high. Though they'd had depositions all morning, they hadn't had a chance to speak outside of case work.

"Hey, do you have a minute?"

Adrian's head whipped up, and he set down his pen. "Of course. What can I help you with?"

She shut the door behind her and took a seat across from him. It was peculiar to see him with the same desk she'd used up until his reappearance. "Um, I wanted to talk about dinner this week. I was planning on lasagna for Sunday. Do you want to come?"

Relaxing in his chair, he folded his hands together on his lap. "Sure, sounds good. I'll bring dessert."

"Perfect, thanks." She cleared her throat, her mind turning back to his recent hospital stay. "Are you feeling better? Dr. Randall mentioned you went to the hospital."

He looked down at the folders on his desk and let out a loud breath. "I'm fine. Just had a heart palpitation."

She cocked her brow. "That doesn't sound good."

"It's not the greatest. Ever since the whole fiasco last year, my heart hasn't been the same." He scratched his ear and avoided her gaze. "After all those surgeries, I can't say I'm surprised. I just have to watch my stress, that's all."

"You're in the wrong line of work." She snorted. "Seriously, Adrian, if you ever need help or someone to go to the doctor with, I'll go with you. As your friend."

He politely smiled. "Thanks, Joce, but being around you only makes my heart beat faster, so it's probably not the best idea." He chuckled. "But I appreciate the offer."

Joci crossed her legs and stared at him. Normally, Adrian wouldn't be so cavalier about his health. He also wouldn't accept "no" for an answer to anything. *Maybe Dr. Randall is right, and he changed for the better.* She hoped so for Brett's sake. He deserved a dad who'd be present. The old Adrian wouldn't have been.

"Now, shifting gears a bit, I heard Cameron is in a bit of trouble." Adrian coughed, but she saw the smile behind his hand.

"Yeah, I wanted to talk to you about that." She pushed up her glasses. "Do you think you can speak with the county attorney's office? It was all a big misunderstanding and—"

Adrian held up his hand, silencing the rest of her plea. "I'll see what I can do." He picked up his cell phone. "Our son deserves to see his mom happy. If Cameron does that, then I won't stand in your way." He lifted the phone to his ear.

Joci stood just as Adrian greeted the county attorney in charge of Cameron's case. She smiled and left him to it. Only after closing the door did she second-guess Adrian's motives. He was cordial and polite almost all the time.

And now he's fixing Cam's problems? It didn't compute, but dwelling on it right then wouldn't help either. *Maybe he's trying to make amends.* She wasn't sure what to believe, but she had a lunch date with Rayna that wasn't going to wait. She was in dire need of Thai food.

She and Rayna chatted over lunch about renting out the empty office to another attorney; they agreed it'd help lower their rent and the cost of the part-time receptionist they'd hired the month prior.

Joci smiled at the woman in her sixties entering the office. Beatrice had a solid work history with law firms. She knew how to run an office, but the retired grandmother simply wanted extra money to spend on her grandchildren. Seeing how they could use the help, she and Rayna had hired her on the spot. It was a little like having a grandmother greet her at work. The older woman even baked and brought pastries each week for the small break room.

Opening her office door, Joci flipped on the light and gasped at the sight in front of her. Sitting on her chair was a bouquet of bright pink peonies. "Aww, who dropped these off?" she called.

Beatrice waddled over and stood in the doorway while Joci sniffed the flowers.

"It was a short blonde lady this morning," she explained, putting on her bifocals. She smiled. "She was the nicest girl and had such pretty red lipstick."

Joci frowned and snatched the note from the bouquet. She only knew one person who fit the description. Beatrice kept droning on, but she wasn't listening anymore.

Roses are red, peonies are pink, danger is closer than you think.

She dropped the card after seeing a lipstick kiss on the bottom. Something Cameron had mentioned about his ex-girlfriend surfaced to the front of her brain. She was obsessed with everything red, which meant the flowers and warning were from Bambina Del Rossi.

Slowly sitting down, Joci rubbed her hands over her thighs, hoping she was wrong. Deep down, she knew she wasn't. She looked up and was grateful Beatrice had returned to her desk to answer a phone call. Deciding it was better to leave the flowers where they were, she took a few photos of the card and vase and sent them to Cameron, then Quinn.

Within ten minutes, Quinn barreled through the front door, nearly scaring Beatrice to an early grave.

"What the hell happened?" he roared, stomping into the office. He glanced around, searching for danger. "Are you okay? Where's Rayna?"

She nodded and stood. "I'm fine, and so is Rayna, but I think Cameron's ex doesn't like me so much." She handed him the card, and Quinn's lips drew into a thin line.

"I warned him she was trouble." He shook his head. "I wondered where she'd run off to after trailing us."

"She followed you guys?" Joci put a hand over her stomach, suddenly in need of antacids. Her one run-in with the blonde bombshell had been creepy enough. This time felt even worse.

Quinn examined the bouquet carefully. "Yep. He said

he'd talk to her about it. Evidently, Bambi didn't like their chat." He walked over to her. Tilting her chin up, he searched her face. "Are you sure you're okay?"

Joci's hands trembled, but she managed to nod. "Yeah, I'll be fine. Just a little unnerved."

Quinn pulled her into a hug and ran his hand over her head. "I would be too."

He held her there for a long minute, and Joci wished it were Cameron instead. She needed his strong arms around her, and it suddenly irked her that he hadn't even responded to her text.

"Have you heard from Cam?"

Detaching from the embrace, Quinn offered her a quizzical look. "No, why?"

"What if Bambi tries to hurt him next?"

"He can handle his own with that one, believe me."

She retreated to the desk and glared at the flowers. "He can, but I'm afraid he won't if Jerry is around. Something doesn't feel right about this. Why would she threaten me if she wasn't planning on doing the same to Cam? Surely, she'd know any threat would piss him off."

"Maybe that's what she wants," he offered. "If Cam acts against her, he might find himself in deep shit with the mob."

She pressed her lips together. Too many scenarios played out in her mind. "Can you track him with his cell phone?"

"I guess, but do you really want to, Joce?" Quinn rested his hands on his hips. "It could get him in more trouble if he's out with Del Rossi."

Grabbing her phone, she called Cameron's number. "Straight to voicemail."

"Never a good sign." He walked to the door. "Let's go."

"Where?"

"Police station. I don't have tracking capabilities here, Joce." He smirked. "I'm a cop, not a mobster."

"Har-har, jerk." She retrieved her purse and locked her office door this time. After letting Beatrice go home early, she followed Quinn to the parking lot. Climbing in her Mercedes, she hoped they'd find Cameron passed out on the couch instead of dead in a ditch somewhere.

CHAPTER SIXTEEN

I can't do it. No matter how many times Bambi yelled at him to pull the trigger, Cameron couldn't—and wouldn't—do it. He stared at the two men on their knees in front of him. He wasn't a killer and he sure as hell wasn't about to become one.

Tossing the gun to the ground, he shook his head. "Nope, not doing it."

Bambi squinted and rolled back her shoulders. "Fine." She shoved him away and scooped up the gun. "I'll finish this." She cocked the gun and aimed.

Cameron lifted her arm at the same time she fired. The bullet hit the side of the old barn nearby, and both men cowered.

"What the hell?" she screamed, turning the gun on him. "You heard Jerry. They're done for. You won't shoot them, so I will."

He gripped her wrist and carefully pointed it toward the ground. "Nobody has to die, Bambi." He nodded to Ulrich and Wong. "I guarantee they've done some shitty stuff and a government agency is looking for them. Let the cops have them." He pried her finger off the trigger and quickly slid the safety in place.

"The hell I will," Bambi hissed, her blue eyes shining hatred. "You went full-on cop, didn't you? How disappointing. I warned Jerry you went straight. Del Rossi doesn't want that. We need the badass Cameron, not this wimpy version."

"Too bad." He managed to free the gun from her entirely. "I don't want to be a badass for Del Rossi anymore. I just want to be good for me and my life." He eyed the fifth person in their party. The bulky assassin didn't say many words. He didn't have to. It surprised Cameron that Charlie hadn't cracked his neck when he failed to kill as ordered.

"You're a waste," she spat, punching him in the nose.

Cameron gritted his teeth but didn't press the issue. He'd never hit a woman, even if Bambi deserved punishment. If Bambi needed to whale on him to get her rocks off, then fine. He'd stand there and take it like a man.

She hooked his jaw next. He had to admit, she'd gotten better over the years. Her jabs weren't weak like he expected.

"I'm done with Del Rossi."

"Not until you kill them." She moved to hit him again, but he lunged out of the way.

"Enough," Charlie growled.

Both Cameron and Bambi paused and swiveled their attention to the tattoo-covered man.

Charlie pushed off from his spot against the barn and tightened a silencer to his gun. Keeping his gaze on Cameron, he popped off two shots. The thud of bodies forced him to look over. Ulrich and Wong were dead.

The mob assassin shoved his gun to the small of his back. "It's done. Let's go." His gruff words sounded out of place among the newly flowering fields.

Bambi instantly stepped away, fear written all over her face. Nobody screwed with the man now standing in front of them.

"But what about—"

Charlie's glare silenced the rest of Bambi's words. He jerked his head toward the SUV, and she scurried to it. "I'll take care of the bodies, but you're not done, Shearer."

Cameron swallowed hard and itched to use the gun in his hands. If only one of them was going to walk away, he'd try his damnedest to beat Charlie to the trigger. Before he could slide his finger over the safety, the hit man swiped the gun away from him.

"Don't make this harder than it has to be." Charlie cocked his gun to Cameron's chest.

Staring into the other man's face, he noticed the mobster had a small tattoo in the dimple of his chin. If he wasn't about to fight for his life, he might've asked about the odd placement.

"Then don't do it. Let me go. Del Rossi will never hear or see me again."

He looked past Charlie but couldn't see anything except plenty of wide, open spaces to hide a body. He wouldn't beg for his life. He'd accepted long ago that death would come at the hands of Del Rossi. He'd just hoped the situation was different and he'd had a chance to say goodbye. *Così è la vita. Such is life.*

Closing his eyes, he braced himself for the inevitable. What he didn't expect was a gunshot to the side.

"We're even," Charlie whispered, shoving him to the ground. Cameron wanted to thank him, but another pop resounded, this time in his left shoulder. Then another to his leg. He hit the dirt hard, the excruciating pain blinding him. He kept his eyes closed and remained motionless.

Warm blood trickled down his body, but Cameron didn't dare move. Not until the SUV left. The car door slammed, and the engine roared to life. He lay there seemingly dead just in case Del Rossi was watching the location.

After a few minutes with no sounds but the wind through the green grass, he reached for the wounds, finding sticky blood drenching his clothes. The pain he could handle. None of the bullets had hit anything vital. He'd live. *If I don't bleed out.* And now he knew without a doubt Jerry didn't want him to be a part-time mobster. Del Rossi wanted all or nothing.

Rolling over, he winced at the searing pain in his side and shoulder. The leg wound wasn't as bad; a graze, from the look of it. He needed to get to a hospital and fast. If he lived long enough to get his life back in place, he had a choice to make. He could roll over and hide while Del Rossi wreaked havoc. Cameron gritted his teeth at his jagged movements. Or he could do exactly what the FBI intended and put Del Rossi to bed for good.

The decision was simple. He didn't back down from trouble.

Digging out his phone, he cringed when the simple act hurt. He'd never complain about cardio day at the gym ever again if he survived.

He dialed the one number he knew would answer.

"Quinn, I've been shot. Call Captain Eicher. She needs to know." His head pounded, the rush of blood quickly draining his thoughts.

"Why? What the hell—?"

Cameron collapsed, and his partner's worried voice scattered across the yard.

***

Another minute ticked by with no change. Joci stared at the clock on the wall and willed time to hurry up. Cameron had been in surgery for an hour. No one had bothered to give her an update since Quinn found Cameron at a foreclosed farm in Adel and brought him to the hospital. After they'd tracked Cameron's cell phone to those coordinates, Quinn told her to go back to work until he knew something more. She'd only agreed so long as he kept her in the loop. *Regretting not going with him right about now.* The only information provided was that he'd been shot. *Three times.*

She practically ran down the courthouse stairs when she'd read the message after her client's arraignment hearing. The twins were fine at home with the nanny, but she let Rayna drive her to the hospital. She was too much of a wreck to get there without crashing into something.

Twisting a strand of hair around her index finger, Joci bobbed her right knee up and down. This had Del Rossi scribbled all over it. Quinn's one word of advice was to keep quiet about the whole thing. She'd shoved his chest when he suggested it, but that only hurt her hand and her patience. She needed answers, but no one save Cameron could provide them. *And he's under the knife at the moment.*

"He's going to be okay, Joce," Rayna comforted, rubbing her hand over Joci's back.

She looked over at her but didn't respond. Keeping calm meant not speaking. She stood and paced. *At least now I know how Cameron felt when I was in delivery.* She took off her glasses and rubbed the bridge of her nose.

The double doors opened, and she turned. To her disappointment, only Adrian rushed through and made his way to her.

"I just heard." He hugged her close and she let herself relax a little. "What happened? Was he working undercover?"

Joci let out a bitter laugh and escaped his arms. "I don't know. It's possible, I guess." She walked over to where Rayna and Quinn sat. "He was on Del Rossi business."

Adrian's brows furrowed. "They wouldn't leave him there to die." His eyes darkened. "Would they?"

"I'd hope not." She sat, then sprang to her feet again. Staying still for more than a minute drove her insane. "Jerry won't answer my calls."

"You called him?" Quinn asked, distress evident in his voice.

"Well, yeah, why wouldn't I?" She saw Quinn and Adrian exchange a look. "What? What aren't you telling me?"

Quinn stood and wrapped an arm around her shoulders. "From the looks of it, Del Rossi meant for Cam to die out there today."

"No!" She whirled away from him. "They adore him."

"But he's been trying to get out of the mob for the last two years, Joce," Adrian inputted. "I don't think Del Rossi liked that. Maybe Cam went too far and they decided to tie up loose ends."

The worried expressions on all three of their faces finally registered. It was more than possible. If Del Rossi was done with Cameron, then she might be next.

"I need to…." She couldn't finish the thought.

Gripping her midsection, she ran to the bathroom and emptied her stomach. Coughing, she flushed the toilet and simply sat on the cool tile floor. All of the warning signs were there but she chose to ignore them. Tears raced down her face until they reached her lips.

"It's my fault," she repeated, bringing up her knees and rocking back and forth. "I pushed him to get out." Her stomach heaved again, and after throwing up, she returned to the floor. In the back of her mind, she knew Cameron had wanted out just as much as she did. Still, it didn't help her conscience.

"Joci, are you in here?" Rayna's voice called in the empty bathroom.

Unlatching the lock, she opened the stall door. "Yes."

Rayna's heels stopped outside the stall. "Oh, sweetie." She knelt and wrapped Joci in a hug. "He's fine."

"You don't know that."

"Yes, I do. The surgeon came out and is looking for you." Rayna pushed back Joci's hair and smiled. "Cameron is alive, and more importantly, awake. Come on, let's go see him."

"Really?" She wiped her nose with the sleeve of her shirt. Rayna nodded enthusiastically, and Joci let out a loud sob before starting to cry all over again. Losing Cameron would eventually destroy her. *But not today.*

***

The sensation of cotton balls in his mouth gradually woke Cameron. His muscles screamed their displeasure when he tried to move. Prying his eyelids open, he swiftly scanned the room. It was empty except for Joci sitting in a chair to his right. He couldn't see her properly thanks to a kink in his neck, but he sensed her presence. The familiar scent of coffee and berries also clued him in that he wasn't alone. He let out a relieved sigh. Quinn had found him. He was alive. *Somehow.*

"Joce," he rasped, instantly hating the small sound of his own voice.

Her head shot up from the magazine in her hands, and she met his gaze. "Oh my God, Cam." She stood and went to hug him, then paused at the plethora of tubes and monitors. Carefully, she leaned over and pressed a kiss to his forehead. "You son of a bitch, you scared me."

He chuckled and winced when it shot a new surge of pain through his body. "Damn, woman, can't you see I'm injured?"

She smirked, and he saw the tears in her hazel eyes. "Yes, and I'm pissed at you for it."

He licked his dry lips, and she offered him a drink. After he sipped the cool water through a straw, he sighed his thanks. "Sorry, I thought I had it under control."

Joci sat on the edge of the bed and brushed his thick hair off his brow. "Did Del Rossi do this?" When he didn't answer, she gasped. "They did."

"Can't say I'm surprised." He shifted, trying to sit up, but found it exceptionally difficult. "They wanted me to kill someone. Two people actually."

"Oh, Cam."

"I couldn't do it." He touched his jaw, still tender from Bambi's punches. "He was supposed to kill me."

Confusion flashed in her eyes. "He sure as hell tried."

"No, he didn't." Cameron laced his fingers in hers. "If Charlie Gambino wants you dead, you die." He kissed the back of her hand. "I guess assassins can have a moral compass too." He chuckled and instantly regretted it.

"Hang on, I'll call for the doctor." She pressed a button nearby, and he was thankful she didn't leave his side. "There." She squeezed his hand. "Why didn't he kill you? I'm not complaining, it just seems odd if those were his orders."

"I saved his ass nine years ago. I'm surprised he remembered." He pinched his brows together.

"You're hard to forget," she said, eyeing the tattoo on his hand.

Cameron reached up and traced her bottom lip. He could handle Joci pissed, but when she cried, he folded like a deck of cards. "I'm okay, babe. I swear."

She shook her head. "No, you're not. Somebody shot you. Multiple times. And they could've…." She let out a shaky breath. "You could've died."

"But I didn't." He offered her a weak smile. She was right on more than one level, but dwelling on it wouldn't do either of them any good. "Nobody is taking me from you."

"What about Jerry?"

"Jerry will be pissed when he finds out I'm alive." He frowned. "Charlie isn't known for the people he lets escape. I've only met him a handful of times, so there's no reason to spare me."

"Well, if I ever meet him, I'll thank him for not killing you."

"He'll deny it."

"Probably." She kissed the tattoo on his wrist. "What're we going to do about Del Rossi?"

"I don't know." Cameron shifted his eyes to the bottom of the bed. It was the one thing that had dominated his thoughts ever since being shot. "I never imagined Jerry would try to murder me, but I guess I pissed him off."

"Or his sister."

She had a point. A very valid one. Jerry threatened bodily harm—and even gave some—but death wasn't something the mob boss would do to him.

"You might be right. If Bambi wants something, she gets her way."

Joci sat up slightly. "She sent flowers to me with a warning."

His nostrils flared, and his heart monitor beeped angrily. "What? When?"

"This morning."

"Shit, I'm sorry." Pulling her closer, he held back his rage at the situation. This was all his fault. Closing his eyes, he thought back to the time he and Bambi crossed paths years ago. She'd gotten her way at his expense. The same could be said about this time around. He didn't have to be a detective to put the clues together.

"I rejected her."

"What?"

He couldn't look away from the IV in his arm. "She offered me a deal. If I slept with her, then I'd be out." He held his breath, waiting for Joci's reply. Surely she'd be livid.

"That bitch!" Joci jostled the bed as she scrambled to her feet, and he sucked in a breath at the pain inadvertently caused.

"Remind me later to never get shot again. It's not fun."

She covered her mouth with her hand. "Oops, sorry. I just can't believe someone would want you dead because you wouldn't sleep with them."

Her brow furrowed in the cutest way, and Cameron grinned. Joci was the best thing in his life. *Her and the boys.*

"Babe, it's okay. It wasn't about sex. Believe me.

Bambi hated me when I told her brothers about the bad shit she'd done over the years." He waved his hand to her. "Guess I'm not very good with women, huh?"

"Maybe not all women." Joci retraced her steps and carefully lay next to him on the hospital bed. "You did win me over."

He kissed the top of her head. "Barely."

"I'd choose you every time." She gently pressed her lips against his, and Cameron wished he wasn't shackled by tubes, hospital walls, and healing gunshot wounds.

"I love you, Joce." He swiped his thumb across her cheek, taking a stray tear with it. Her hazel eyes held more than tears, and all he wanted to do was spirit them away from anything remotely involving a mob. She deserved the best, and that's what he'd give her.

"I love you too." She kissed him again, and he made up his mind that he'd do exactly that. Del Rossi would pay for putting them through hell.

***

Joci glanced between the woman in a captain's uniform and Cameron on the hospital bed. She knew the truth. All of it. Her first reaction was to curse her fiancé out, but she opted against it since Captain Eicher and Agent Stevens with the FBI were also in the room.

"So, you've been working undercover with the FBI and police and you want to pretend you're dead?" She didn't like the words even as she regurgitated them.

Cameron nodded, an uneasy expression on his face.

"Yeah."

"This is crazy."

Agent Stevens flipped through the accordion-style file on his lap. "I spoke in length with the FBI director, and he wants Del Rossi. 'Anything to get them' were his words. If Del Rossi believes Cameron is dead, their guard will be down. At least when it comes to you, Joci. Jerry won't suspect anything if you contact him."

Joci traced her engagement ring with her index finger, trying to sort out the suggested plan. It made sense, but she wasn't sure she could pull something like this off. She wasn't trained for combat unless it involved a courtroom.

"But if you aren't comfortable with this, Joce, it's okay. We'll figure something else out." Cameron rubbed his thumb over her hand. "The original plan didn't include my death, so we've already had to improvise."

The constant whir of the hospital monitors filled the silence. If she asked Cameron for a favor, he wouldn't think twice. She couldn't expect him to do that if she wasn't willing herself.

"I'll do it, but we need to keep you safe, Cam."

"How about the penthouse at Petosa Law?" a new voice suggested.

Joci looked over her shoulder to see Quinn and Rayna at the door. Unless Rayna had suddenly grown another head, Adrian was there too.

"That will work. It's the safest place for him," Quinn said as they came into the room.

Agent Stevens nodded. "I can station an agent or two

on the building. It would make contact easier too, since the building is secure."

Rayna closed the door. "Okay then, what do you need the rest of us to do?"

Captain Eicher reviewed the group now filling the hospital room. "Officer Quinn, you be my DMPD contact to bring the plan together. Unfortunately, I'm unable to pass any other information along to Mr. Petosa and Ms. Alley."

"Sure, we understand." Rayna patted Joci's arm. "Just want to help in any way possible."

They all looked to Adrian. He cleared his throat and nodded. "Yes, me too."

"Great." Agent Stevens stood and moved toward the exit. "Shearer, once you're settled, I'll bring the FBI and DMPD along to form a new plan. Officer Quinn, make sure he stays alive until then."

Quinn's back straightened, and he nodded curtly. "Yes, sir."

Joci caught Captain Eicher's smirk before she smothered it and followed the FBI agent.

"And Ms. Dorous, act the grieving fiancée. Jerry and the rest of his mafia will be watching you the moment you leave this hospital." Captain Eicher closed the file and quickly left in silence.

"Then I guess I shouldn't buy any *Get Better Soon* balloons from the gift shop downstairs?" Rayna teased, but only Quinn chuckled.

"Not this time, Ray." Joci pushed up her glasses and glanced around the room. They were all in danger due to

Del Rossi. It was up to her—along with a few government agencies—to corner the mob before they consumed them all.

"Can I have a few minutes with Cam, please?"

"Shit, sorry, yeah. We'll get out of your hair." Quinn made a round-up signal with his hand and all but herded Rayna and Adrian from the room. "I'll call you later," he said, shutting the door.

"What's wrong?" Cameron asked, patting the edge of the bed.

"I'm scared." She longed to cozy up next to him, but if she did that, she wasn't sure if she'd ever leave. "I don't like the idea of you alone."

He glanced to his surroundings. "Believe me, I won't be alone. The nurses check on me every half hour."

"I don't like pretending that Del Rossi's hitman killed you either." Tears built up in her eyes and fogged her glasses. "I can't lose you."

He waved her over, but she didn't budge. "Joce, I'm literally attached to tubes and can't haul you into my arms and pin you down like I want to." His brown eyes pleaded with her even more than his words. "Please come here."

She didn't need to be asked twice. Carefully, she settled beside him on the bed. She opened her lips to argue her case, but he was there, consuming them with his mouth. Tears dripped down her cheeks the more he kissed her, coaxing her with the silent words on his lips.

"I'm not dead, and I won't be for a very long time." He wiped away a tear with his thumb. "I don't like putting you in danger either, babe. It's what I've been trying to avoid ever since meeting you. And I sure as hell don't like to pretend I'm dead." He kissed another tear on her cheek. "But in order to get rid of Del Rossi, we have to."

"I know." Her eyes dropped to the clean, white sheets. "I'll miss you."

"Well, you do work eight hours a day at minimum in the same building that I'll be stuck in." He tilted up her chin, and she recognized the mischievous gleam in his brown eyes. "Maybe you'll come visit me more this time around." His lips trailed over her neck. "Especially since you know how good I'll—"

"All right, Mr. Shearer, let's check your vitals," a cheerful nurse said, bursting into the room. She eyed Joci warily at first, given how close she was to his bandages, but then smiled. "I'm glad you're keeping an eye on this one. He's quite the looker. Has the whole second floor talking about those tattoos and pretty eyes."

Joci moved to let the nurse work and watched Cameron. A red tint covered his cheeks at the nurse's compliments. "He's definitely a catch." She winked at him, and he grinned. "And all mine."

"Good thing. I'd have to hide him away from the crowd of nurses sure to beat down his door."

The nurse kept babbling about the hospital and how good-looking Cameron was, but Joci didn't hear any of it. She was too focused on maintaining her fiancé's devoted gaze. It was all she needed to solidify her decision.

CHAPTER SEVENTEEN

This idea was crazy and not what she wanted for her Wednesday. Joci straightened the hem of her skirt one last time and inhaled deeply. Catching her reflection in the rearview mirror, she took in the perfect makeup and slightly red eyes. She'd honestly thought Cameron was a goner until she saw him out of surgery.

The police chief had made a visit to his room shortly after that. Evidently, he was extremely interested in hearing why the Del Rossi mob wanted Cameron dead now and if his cover had been blown. The chief made it clear that Cameron's suspension was lifted, but he'd be watched closely due to not including the police department from the start. It was more than she'd hoped for.

The FBI outfitted her with everything she needed for her first visit with Jerry Del Rossi. An agent was assigned to her for daily protection, something she was familiar with. A small camera was built into the barrette holding back her hair. The location was perfect and stylish. *Never thought I'd say that about law enforcement.*

Adjusting her glasses, she prepared herself to get out of the car and do her part of the plan. In her own way, she was excited to be part of this operation. Her uneasy stomach knew better, though. This wasn't a heated debate about criminal charges. This was real life and death. No one liked involving her, but she didn't have a choice. She wanted Del Rossi out of Iowa, and she'd suck up her fears to get it done.

Joci took a steadying breath and glanced at the bodyguard near the hotel entrance. Her part was the glue of the operation that held the rest together. Cameron was supposedly dead, and she needed to play the forlorn fiancée seeking help.

Fluffy clouds hiding the sun's spring rays met her outside the warm car. *Rain would be more suitable.* She trudged across the parking lot and nodded once to the burly men at the entrance.

The newly refurbished hotel smelled clean. *Too clean.* She didn't want to think about the reasons why bleach was stronger than the disinfectant scent. Del Rossi wasn't a caring mob; they were relentless and brutal. How easily they offed Cameron reiterated it.

Reaching the last room, she let the two bodyguards pat her down before bidding her entrance. The moment she stepped through the doors, her mouth dropped open. Plastic sheets covered the floor and one wall. They were white, but for how long, she didn't know.

"Joci," Jerry greeted, moving toward her. His brows were drawn together, a pitiful expression written on his chubby face. "I'm sorry to hear about Cameron." He enclosed her hands within his sweaty ones. "He was one of my favorites."

Tears welled, and she tried to hold them back. She was staring into the face of the man who didn't give a damn about anyone but himself. If it meant he killed a hundred people to satisfy one, the man would order it.

"Thanks. I still can't believe he's gone." She wiped away the stray tears.

"If there is anything I can do, please let me know." He handed her a tissue. If anyone stepped in, they'd think the scene was fatherly, but Joci knew better.

"Can you find out who did this?" She followed him to a desk and set of chairs. "I have a few police contacts, and they can help if needed."

"Of course, but police won't be necessary. I started investigating upon hearing of the horrible accident." He snapped his fingers, and a folder seemingly materialized in his hands. "Here's what I found."

Taking the offering, Joci opened it and frowned. It was blank. "Um, there's nothing in here."

Jerry chuckled. "Yes, because in order to get information, I need information."

Joci clenched her hands around the folder. He was attempting to manipulate the circumstances of Cameron's death. It was sick and twisted and exactly what she expected from the mobster.

He leaned over and bopped her on the nose with his index finger. "I think we can come to an agreement of sorts."

"What kind of agreement?"

"Your legal services for my less than legal ones."

Joci swallowed at the insinuation. He wanted to trade her life for information about Cameron's death. *Scumbag.* Any other time, she'd refuse Jerry. He'd asked on multiple occasions for her to join Del Rossi as their legal counsel. Each time, she'd declined. This time, though, the Feds and police wanted her to give in.

"Okay, I think I can do that. I need to know what happened to Cameron, and if you can help, I'd appreciate it."

A cunning smile crept over Jerry's face. "Wonderful." He clasped her hands. "My men will be sent immediately to investigate. They should have something by the end of the week." He kissed her cheek. "I'll be in touch then, yes?"

Joci fought back the bile rising in her throat. Being this close to the man who brought so much pain to so many families made her fingers itch to claw his eyes out. "That'd be great, thank you."

"Anything for Cameron's girl." He stood, bringing her with him. "And in the meantime, I have a few cases I need you to take care of." One of his men handed him a large folder. "These indiscretions really don't need to see the light of day. Think you can make it happen?"

Taking the folder, she nodded. It was heavier than expected. Crime didn't sleep or so it seemed. "I'm on it."

Jerry wrapped her in a hug. "Del Rossi will take care of the funeral expenses. Just let me know."

Joci froze before she could stop it. The idea of any

mobster around Cameron sent her blood to ice water. She managed to sniffle and hoped she pulled off the act well enough. When she pulled back and looked into Jerry's face, she didn't see any indication that he sensed a farce.

"Thanks, but I already consented to a cremation."

He nodded. "Of course, I understand. Send me the bill, nonetheless. It's the least we can do. We'll arrange for a memorial as well."

Walking toward the exit, she managed a small smile. "Thanks, Jerry. You always looked out for us."

He placed a hand over his heart and smiled grimly. After nodding, she left, eager to be rid of the place. The air in the hallway was sweet compared to the intense scent of cigars and sweat in the room. A loud cry of pain echoed behind her, and she picked up her pace. Whatever was happening in the hotel, she wanted nothing to do with it.

Attaining the outdoors once more, Joci made it to her car before retching in the nearby bushes. *You can do this*, she repeated to herself. Any other case, she'd simply roll back her shoulders and put on a brave face. This was different. It wasn't a random person she was saving this time around. More than her future hung in the balance. Tangling with mobsters never felt more dangerous. *It'll be worth it.* She clung to that hope.

***

Reviewing the security camera footage from the last week, Cameron jotted down a few more notes, then tossed the pen aside. He looked around the massive penthouse and groaned.

He'd hoped staying in the Petosa apartment wouldn't last long, but he was wrong.

He carefully stood and braced himself for the imminent pain. Sure enough, it flooded him once he was upright. The pain medicine only numbed so much. The rest was up to his body to heal itself. After he'd been discharged, the FBI placed him under protective service at the Petosa loft. Joci visited daily, sometimes more than once, but it wasn't the same as being home with her.

"Find anything good in those?" Quinn asked from the kitchen.

"Not really. It's mostly members coming and going." Cameron hobbled to the kitchen and sat on one of the barstools. He really hated Gambino for shooting him in the leg. It made life more complicated than necessary. "When will we have the tail footage?"

Quinn shrugged and grabbed a bagel from the toaster. "Dunno. My guess is by the end of the week. Feds like to crawl right up in their target's ass and get all the good stuff." He chuckled and grabbed the cream cheese from the fridge.

"Super." He watched Quinn slather on way too much blueberry cream cheese, then bite into the bagel. His best friend was a constant companion when he was off shift. Naturally, the FBI had a protection detail for him when Quinn wasn't around, but Cameron missed being out in the world.

"These walls are my prison. Again. I thought it'd never happen."

"Yeah, but this time, you didn't do anything wrong."

Quinn pointed his bagel at him. "Well, sort of. You're giving up Del Rossi. No one but them will blame you for it."

He ran his fingers through his hair and nodded. "I know. I hate being away from Joce and the boys."

"They visit. She brings them up twice a day at least."

"It's not the same, Quinn." He rested his forehead on the marble counter. "Seeing them a couple times isn't the same as being able to take Levi and Brett to the park or go out to a movie with Joci." He closed his eyes and tried to not think about the danger they were in because of him.

"Joci is okay," Quinn said, as if reading his thoughts.

Propping his chin on his hand, Cameron gave him a pointed look. "No, she's not."

"She is. Believe me about that, if nothing else. DMPD and the FBI have someone watching her at all times."

"As does Jerry."

"Yeah, we've had to adjust her security because of it, but Del Rossi hasn't caught on yet. She's keeping her head down and doing exactly what Jerry wants her to do." Quinn finished off half the bagel and grabbed the remaining piece. "Nothing's going to happen."

"I wish I could believe you. I really do." He stood and made his way back to the living room. The clock on the wall struck noon, and his pace quickened. Joci would bring the boys up over her lunch break.

Thanks to Adrian—whom Cameron remained wary of— the firm opened a day care for their employees on the second floor. While Joci still kept their nanny, she opted to take the boys to work as often as possible and only utilized the older woman when court ran late. It gave him little relief. Del Rossi continued to be involved in his boys' lives. Until they got rid of the mob altogether, Cameron wouldn't be safe, and neither would the people he loved.

"So, can I call you Ghost?" Quinn asked. "You know, because you're dead but not dead."

"Try and see what happens," he replied with a smirk.

"How about Specter? That one is kind of badass." Quinn scratched his chin. "On the other hand, you're not very badass."

Cameron chuckled and shook his head. Ever since his near-death experience, Quinn hadn't relented in giving him shit. It was nice in a way to see that nothing had really changed. A select few people knew about his "fatal" gunshot wounds, but there hadn't even been a grand funeral. Just a simple memorial with enough Del Rossi members to make it legitimate.

Naturally, the FBI splashed the news in the local papers to make it appear true. He didn't care all that much. Everyone he cared about was aware he wasn't dead. It was all he wanted. Plus, any of the people he'd pissed off during his Del Rossi years could safely put their vendetta to bed.

For now.

Once Jerry was behind bars, his testimony would be the key in putting the man away for life. He'd need more than witness protection to keep the remaining Del Rossi siblings at bay. Agent Stevens was positive the FBI could indict without his help, but they also didn't want him scurrying off to never be heard from again. No matter which way

Cameron looked at it, he was screwed.

"How long will this take?"

Quinn sobered momentarily. "No clue. Hopefully, not too long or Joci might forget about you."

Cameron flipped him the bird. "You're a jackass."

"Yeah, well, you knew this, partner."

"Don't you have some other person you can harass? Like an auburn-haired attorney?"

Wiggling his brows, Quinn grinned. "Maybe."

"I suggest you focus on her. Joce is taken."

Quinn walked to the edge of the kitchen. "I know, man. Just giving you shit. It's better than the alternative, right? Nobody likes being lonely. Especially up here." He glanced around. "Honestly, I'm afraid I'd break something."

"Not like the firm can't replace it." Cameron went back to the kitchen and grabbed a bottle of water.

"True." Quinn checked his phone. "Shift's about to start. Do you want me to grab you anything for dinner?"

What he wanted was Joci, but he doubted Quinn could and would provide that delicacy. "How about a cheesesteak? Is that on your way?"

"It is now." Quinn's green eyes lit up, and he nodded enthusiastically. "That sounds fucking amazing. I'll pick up a couple and drop them off."

"Thanks." He chuckled at Quinn all but drooling. "Try to save me one, yeah?"

The front door beeped, and he expectantly glanced to the entrance. When all he saw was Adrian, he paused his joyful reaction.

"Adrian." He sat on the sofa and grabbed the remote.

"Hey, Cam. Hey, Quinn." Adrian came into the room and loosened his tie. "Joci will be up in a few minutes."

"Great."

Quinn patted the counter. "I gotta run. Catch you later." He waved, the door beeping his exit.

"We should talk," Adrian began once the door shut.

Glancing up from the TV, Cameron cocked an eyebrow. "About what?"

"Joci and the boys."

"What about them?"

Adrian draped his jacket over a chair. "I want to take them away after Joci finishes her role in taking down Del Rossi. The firm can cover her clients until a conviction is entered."

Cameron tossed the remote to the cushion beside him. It made sense. They didn't deserve to be at risk while Jerry awaited a federal trial. Still, it didn't feel right in his soul. Not seeing them every day hurt enough, but a trip without him would be worse.

"Where would you take them?"

"Ireland." Adrian's blue eyes took on a faraway gleam. "I have family there and they'd be safe until this is all over."

Cameron steepled his fingers over his nose. Ireland would be far enough away. He even knew a few men in a motorcycle club over there who could keep tabs on them.

"Whatever it takes to keep my family out of harm's way," he finally said. He hated the words as soon as they slipped out. Joci was safer with him. His family was safe when he was there to protect them. *Or so I thought.*

"All right, I'll speak to her about it later." Adrian's face looked a mite too bright at the news. "You should too. She won't do anything unless you're okay with it."

Cameron returned his focus to the sports show. He heard the telltale sign of Adrian leaving and let out a loud breath. Resting his head on the back of the couch, he stared at the ceiling. He'd always do what was best for Joci and his boys. *Even if it means sending them away.*

***

"I don't like how much you're lying to everyone," Rayna said, following Joci to the next courtroom.

"Shh." Joci pulled her friend closer and smiled at a passing bailiff. Once they were clear of the officer, she glared at Rayna. "I'm not lying, I'm helping the police catch a mob."

Rayna's gray eyes rolled. "Not what I was talking about."

"Oh, you mean Cam."

"Dur."

Joci slid over on a bench in the back of Judge Scott's courtroom. Rayna gracefully plopped beside her. They'd ridden together from their office earlier and already she regretted it. The morning started off perfectly fine when they stopped by a local coffee shop for some caffeine. It went downhill rather quickly afterward.

When Rayna spotted not one but three cars following them, she freaked out. *There's a reason I didn't tell her about them.* The morning would've gone smoothly, but her friend was too perceptive to let anything pass her.

"Joce, everyone here thinks you recently lost the love of your life," Rayna whispered, looking around. "When in actuality, he's on the top floor of Petosa Law. And you're going on business as usual."

"You know that's not the case, Ray. For Cam's safety, I have to play this act. I don't like it at all either."

Opening her legal pad, Joci reviewed her notes about the cases in this courtroom. They were Del Rossi ones. The clients she couldn't refuse lest Jerry get wind of a trap.

Thinking back to her powwow with the FBI and DMPD, she reminded herself of her role.

"Clean up his messes, but make sure you take the evidence directly to Bernard Del Rossi," Agent Stevens stressed during the meeting.

"We'll get a wire on you right before you leave," Captain Eicher added.

"But above all, be safe. None of this is worth your life," Cameron said, rubbing his thumb across her hand.

That had been last week. A total of three weeks had come and gone since Cameron's injury. Both agencies tailed her, plus Del Rossi. Jerry didn't trust her, and he shouldn't. She'd only met with him twice since the conception of the plan. Both times, she picked up a little intel that would help the growing case against him. It wasn't enough, according to the FBI. The state had plenty, but Joci couldn't hang up her act just yet.

Joci looked over to see Rayna applying lip gloss. She couldn't tell her friend everything even though she wanted to.

Keeping Rayna out of the loop secured her safety. Quinn appreciated the thought, or so he'd said yesterday when he met her at the Petosa apartment.

"We should get enough to indict soon," she finally said to Rayna. "Afterwards, Cam and I will figure it all out."

"You said that two weeks ago." The slender woman fluffed her auburn hair and straightened her jade necklace. "I'm worried about you, Levi, and Brett. I'm not the only one."

Joci met her gaze. "Who, Adrian or Quinn?"

"Er, well, both, but I was talking about Adrian." Rayna pulled out her cell phone and replied to a message before continuing. "Adrian came to our office on Tuesday— probably to see you—and told me about going to Ireland. He's right too. I think you should go now before this shit blows up. Maybe explore the Emerald Isle. If it was me, I wouldn't even pack. I'd just grab my passport and wave goodbye."

Ireland. Joci gritted her teeth. She'd blatantly ignored Adrian's pleas to take an impromptu trip to the land of his ancestors. It wouldn't look out of place, since Brett was his son, after all. No one would bat an eyelash, not even Jerry himself. Everyone not privy to Cameron's status all expected her to shack back up with Adrian anyhow.

Taking out her pen, she clicked it repeatedly. It annoyed her how quickly people got over Cameron's death and practically shoved her into Adrian's lap. She shook her head. *Just because a woman has kids and is alone doesn't mean she needs a man.*

"I'm considering it," she said when Rayna poked her with a bony finger. Rayna tilted her head to the side and pouted her lips. "Okay, okay, more than considering it. The thing is, I can't leave Cam alone here to fight this battle."

"It's his to fight, Joce. He's the one who was in the mob. Not you."

"Maybe, but without the mob, we wouldn't be together. Jerry helped us out—"

"And also blackmailed you both."

She frowned. "Yeah, true. But I'm involved in the Del Rossi mob, Ray, whether I want to be or not. I won't leave Cameron to fend for himself. It's all he's done his entire life. He thought Del Rossi was his family and look what they did to him. His parents were no different. I'm his family now. I won't abandon him like everyone else."

Rayna stared at her for a long minute. Finally, she wrapped her arms around Joci's shoulders and hugged her tight. "I hope someday I find a person who loves me as passionately as you do Cam."

Joci patted Rayna's arm and hugged her back. "You will, Rayna. Who knows, maybe you already did."

"Ms. Dorous, are you ready for your status conference or do you need a moment?" Judge Scott asked from the front of the room.

Whipping her head forward, she quickly stood. "No, thank you, Your Honor, we can proceed." She offered Rayna a quick grin, then walked to the attorney desks.

Pushing up her glasses, Joci couldn't remember all the details of the hearing, but she did manage to drum up a dismissal. Normally, her hearings weren't so easy. She nodded once to the county attorney, who in turn offered a small grin. They were being watched, so the theatrics were necessary. The FBI had reached out to the county attorney's office and managed to secure dismissals for all of the cases Del Rossi tossed her way. They'd get them all in the end on federal charges anyhow.

She lifted her eyes and glimpsed a man clad in black leave the room. *Probably to tell Jerry.* Del Rossi's man would get out of jail later in the day, and he'd be instrumental in the state's case against the mob. Her credibility with Jerry strengthened with each case she won.

Rayna was up next, and Joci took the free time to scan through her work emails. One was from the Petosa Board regarding an upcoming meeting. She rubbed her lips together. *Cutting ties with Petosa Law might be easier after this whole mafia fiasco is over.* She added the meeting to the calendar on her phone and read the next email from Adrian.

After replying about covering an upcoming hearing, she pulled up the messaging app. As badly as she wanted to text Cameron, the agencies had told her not to. Something about Del Rossi still monitoring his number. Her thumbs hovered over the keyboard, a photo of him and the boys attached to the contact. He wasn't gone. She knew that. But not calling him anytime she wanted was strange. Sure, she could visit him, and no one would think twice because the firm hid plenty of clients there, but it wasn't the same.

She noticed a new email with a photo taken by the day

care and smiled at the cheesy grins on Brett's and Levi's faces. They looked more like Adrian and Cameron each passing day. She saved the photo on her phone and made a note to show Cameron later. Adrian had access to the notifications too, so she wouldn't bother sending it to him.

Joci watched the screen dim, a photo of her small family as the wallpaper. She missed Cameron. Not just in a physical way—which was up there—but in an every-day-hang-out kind of way. They had their ebbs and flows like any couple, but she'd take those any day over being apart from him.

She received a text message from Adrian about grabbing dinner with the boys. After accepting, she thought over the last few weeks. Oddly enough, she trusted Adrian more since Cameron's accident. He came by the house to help with the boys and even dropped off groceries a time or two. The FBI thought his coming and going would be good for her safety, and she couldn't disagree.

He was incredible with Brett and Levi. Always ready to play and tickle them. He wasn't the best when it came to mealtime, but she had to admire his dedication even if he ended up with food everywhere.

She smirked, recalling how the twins fell asleep on Adrian the other night. She couldn't help but snap a picture after he fell asleep. He wasn't the old Adrian she knew or even the man from two years ago. Somehow, he was more mature and better than his old self.

Someday, the boys would want to know their origin story and if they saw Cam and Adrian as their dads, surely it wouldn't be such a shock. It was surreal to see Adrian in that light again. She'd never thought she'd get over his betrayal, but a part of her was trying. Loving him again wouldn't happen except in his role as a dad.

"Joce, you ready to go?" Rayna asked, bringing her to the present.

The time flashed on her phone, and she gathered her items. "Sorry, yeah. I got sidetracked."

The two women made their way to the next courtroom and carried on for the next three hours until both were mentally and physically depleted. They rested on the benches outside courtroom 404 after the last hearing. Rayna slipped off her heels and massaged her left foot while they sat in the hallway. Thankfully, the hearing was the last on the docket for the day, so no one else meandered their area.

"I could use a pitcher of margaritas and about ten shrimp tacos," Rayna said, rolling her neck from side to side.

Joci flexed her toes in her pink heels. "Yeah, these puppies won't last through a Rayna-style happy hour. I need slippers, a glass of wine, and Chinese takeout. That's my version of happy hour lately." She laughed when her friend let out a dramatic gasp. "But alas, I'm meeting Adrian at Zombie Burger with the boys in half an hour, so no happy hour in my future."

"Hmm, they have spiked shakes there. Maybe I should go too."

"The more the merrier."

Rayna's phone rang, and she fumbled with it before silencing the ringtone. A red tint crept on her cheeks, and

Joci couldn't resist.

"And who did you just silence, Ms. Alley?"

"No one."

Joci stood and peeked around to make sure no one was nearby. The coast was clear in all directions. "Uh-huh, sure." She spotted the phone on the bench and quickly swiped it. "Come and get it."

Rayna screeched, running after her with only her hosiery between her and the marble flooring.

"Give it back, Joci!"

Running in heels wasn't the best idea, but Joci couldn't help but notice she was faster than Rayna even with the three-inch wedges. "Not until I see who you're sexting."

"Oh my God, I don't sext!"

Joci chuckled and kept moving down the hallway, scrambling to open the iPhone. "You don't even lock it? Amateur."

"Joci, I swear to God, if you don't give it back…."

Chancing a glance back, Joci giggled at the determined look on Rayna's face. "Then you *do* have something to hide. Let's see, shall we open the photos app and see if there're any racy ones?"

Rayna had caught up to her by then, both hands grabbing at the phone. Joci managed to keep her at bay long enough to swipe at the photos. She wasn't disappointed either when one of the snapshots was of Rayna and Quinn looking rather cozy. Before she could fully scroll to the next one, pink nails dug into her palm and she released the device.

"My, my, what did I see?" she taunted good-naturedly.

"A photo of you and Officer Quinn." She tsked and chuckled at Rayna's wild hair due to their unexpected jaunt around the courthouse. Her best friend was too fun to tease, especially about guys.

"We hang out," Rayna rushed to say. "Nothing wrong with that."

Joci leaned against the sturdy railing overlooking the floors below and watched Rayna rapidly scroll through the phone. "No, there's not, but I would be interested in seeing the next photo in that series. I'd bet a round of tequila you and Quinn were much, much closer."

She made a kissing sound, and Rayna's face turned red when she looked at something behind Joci. Turning slightly, she met the curious gaze of their subject of conversation.

"Oh, hey, Quinn."

The man outfitted in full police uniform looked between the two of them. "I, uh, was grabbing a search warrant when I heard some shrieks, so I thought I'd check it out." A boyish grin covered his face. "Should've known it was just the two of you messing around."

Rayna patted down her hair. "Yeah, no big deal. All good here. Just girls being girls." She smiled, but Joci noticed it was more nervous than anything.

"Should I give you two a few minutes?" she offered when Quinn didn't drop Rayna's gaze.

If she could capture the way they looked at each other and replay it later, they'd have to admit to feelings for each other.

***

"It's so obvious," she told Adrian an hour later while they waited on their food. Levi and Brett were munching on puffy cereal in their high chairs, squealing every now and then when they didn't get a refill soon enough.

"Quinn and Rayna are adorably fighting something that rhymes with dove." She poured more cereal for Brett, and Levi immediately reached over and grabbed his brother's food.

Adrian sipped his water, and a smile crept over his cheeks. "Is somebody playing matchmaker?"

"No need! They're already in love. They won't accept it for some reason." She picked up a sippy cup that Brett knocked to the floor. "I literally stood there for a full minute while they looked into each other's eyes all cute like." She snorted. "I mean, honestly, who does that?"

"We used to," he said, clearing his throat.

Joci looked up and was relieved he didn't search out her gaze. Every so often, he'd make a comment about them, but would never follow up on it. She was grateful he let it rest, but would rather him not say anything at all.

"So, how's everything going with your cases?" he asked as their food arrived.

She licked her lips at the enormous burger topped with fried jalapenos, caramelized onions, bacon, guacamole, chipotle mayo, and cheese. The waiter set a basket of fries with homemade dipping sauce between them. Brett reached for one and wailed when he couldn't grab the basket.

Adrian handed each boy a fry and smirked at their exploration of the crispy food.

"Good, I guess. As much as it can." She took a bite and pointed to him.

"Mine are fine too," he replied with a grin before enjoying his barbeque burger concoction. "Having some issues with one of the clients. He wants to go to trial and also testify, which would be detrimental."

"Clients. They think they know best." She smiled around a fry and glanced at the small restaurant.

People didn't come to Zombie Burger to get a boring burger. They came to get something out there. Sometimes way, way, way out there. She sipped her zombie unicorn shake and wondered how she survived without this place. Wax zombies stood at every door, and murals of local sports teams-turned-zombies stood out on the walls. All in all, it was the perfect combination of all things Joci never thought she'd like while eating. That didn't stop her, though. It didn't stop anyone.

"I was thinking, maybe you can bring Brett and Levi over sometime for a sleepover."

She lifted her brows.

"And you, of course." He wiped his hands on a napkin. "I've just never had the experience."

"They sleep through the night, Adrian." She eyed her burger. "Nothing exciting happens now. Four months ago, yes, but these days they sleep like truckers." She tickled Brett's bare feet. The little troublemaker always wiggled socks off. Today was no different.

"Ah, sure." His face fell slightly, and he went back to work on his food.

"But I have a dentist appointment next week, so maybe you can watch the boys for me?" she offered.

His blue eyes turned to her. "Really?"

"Sure. It's Wednesday at five o'clock. If you want to pick them up from day care, I'll get them on the way home."

"That will work." He pulled out his phone. "My last hearing is at three in the afternoon. I can take them back to my place and make dinner if you want."

Joci popped a jalapeño in her mouth and nodded. "Sounds good."

She met his gaze and melted just a little at the trust there. Adrian wasn't a bad guy. Not when it boiled down to it. Over the last month, he'd earned more of her respect than she imagined.

He handed the boys each another fry, despite the fact that the first ones were mush on their high chairs.

"Aw, those guys are absolutely adorable," the waitress said, stopping by their table to refill the glasses with water. "They're miniatures of you both." She patted Levi's curly head, then walked away.

"They are, you know," Adrian said quietly. He reached over and grabbed the bill.

"It's a little uncanny but cute too." She smiled at Brett, then Levi. Both babies reached for her, and she couldn't resist peppering them with kisses. She hated that Cameron was all but locked away in a tower, but having this time with Adrian was good too.

"So, don't take this the wrong way, but why did you choose to come home when you did?"

The fry paused at his lips. "What?"

"The timing of your arrival—second arrival, whatever—is suspicious." She didn't want to toy with words, and it was the number-one question she hadn't asked but wanted to.

"I don't understand. I came home because I wanted to see my son. And you." His blue eyes turned a shade darker, her words seemingly wounding him.

"It's just…. Cameron's ex-girlfriend shows up the exact same day that I start work again after maternity leave and you're my co-counsel. I've been wondering ever since if maybe you knew Bambi Del Rossi."

Adrian sat back and crumpled his napkin from his lap. "You think I'm plotting with a psychopath so we each get the person we want?"

The food on her plate suddenly didn't look very appetizing. "Adrian—"

"Well, I'm not, Joce. I never wanted to be J.J.'s puppet last year." He lowered his voice. "I didn't have a choice, but I do now, and I want to be here."

She sipped her shake. "I had to ask. You understand, right? I need to protect my sons and myself."

Running both hands through his hair, he sighed. "I get it. You don't trust easily, and I haven't exactly been dad of the year or the best partner when it comes to life or law." He reached over and squeezed her hand. "But I need you to understand that I would do anything for you, Joci. Anything to keep you and our son safe."

Regret washed over her. His eyes spoke all she needed to see. The mob hadn't broken him; changed him a little, but he was the same beneath it all. Why it took her so long to realize sent her stomach to a nosedive. She didn't want to believe it. Hating Adrian was easier than being friends again.

"I know, I'm sorry."

"I'm sorry I gave you a reason to doubt me."

The waitress dropped off the receipt, giving their conversation time to digest. Joci smiled over to the twins, who were happily mashing fries on their trays.

"Honestly, I didn't know when I was coming home until I got on the plane." He loosened the top button of his dress shirt. "I just had this feeling like it was time. And I thought maybe you would let me in again. Not in the way we used to be, but as Brett's dad. I realize it's tough, but I appreciate your willingness to let me try."

"The past hurts, Adrian, but I believe you never meant to harm me or anyone I love. As more time goes by, I think we can be a functional modern family." She reached over and snagged a paper napkin before Levi could stuff it in his mouth. "You, me, Cameron, Brett, and Levi. You told Cam you wanted that when the boys were born. I want it too."

"Then I'll do my best to make sure we can still have it." He took out his wallet and put away his card. "And truthfully, I don't like people named after Disney characters, so I'd never be friends with someone named Bambi."

Rolling her eyes, Joci started prepping the boys to leave. It was a relief to hear Adrian's side of her crazed imaginings. Even though she'd never trust him with her life, after hearing his explanation, she felt more comfortable around him. At least a little here and there.

"I have a few cases I need to draft pleadings on before these guys go to bed. Do you want to come over and watch them for me?"

Adrian stood and grabbed Levi from the booster seat. The curly-haired baby bopped Adrian's nose and giggled when he dramatically reacted.

"I'd say that's a yes."

CHAPTER EIGHTEEN

Cameron pressed his forehead against the large glass window overlooking the bustling city below. *Joci is somewhere down there.* She'd recently left, the twins in tow, and he itched to go with her. A few kisses here and there weren't cutting it anymore. Sure, they had some alone time, but it wasn't the same as having the freedom to visit her at the office and hike up her skirt before her next hearing. Plus, his gunshot wounds weren't healing fast enough for him to do much when it came to his fiancée.

His phone rang from the coffee table, and he quickly grabbed it. A distraction was definitely in order.

"What's up?"

"Joce is meeting up with Jerry tonight. She should get the last bit of information needed before the FBI can arrest him," Quinn said from the other end.

"Are you sure? I've heard that before." He walked toward the small gym area just off the main door. Plenty of hours had been spent with those weights over the last two weeks. Between interviews with the FBI and DMPD, he'd had plenty of frustration to let loose afterwards. The only bad part was he couldn't exercise like he wanted. The doctors had put him on a strict physical therapy routine that did very little to alleviate stress. *Probably makes it worse.*

"I sure as hell hope so." Quinn paused, and squealing tires echoed. "They want you there too."

"What? Why?" He brushed his free hand through his hair. "Won't I put Joci in danger?"

"Not if you stick to the FBI truck."

"All right. Are you picking me up?"

"Yep. See you at nineteen hundred hours."

Cameron hung up without signing off. He'd helped make the plan. Joci would hand over more cases that had been swept under the rug for the sake of Del Rossi trusting her. The FBI would swarm the location, arresting both of them to save Joci's reputation. He'd insisted on it. Any blowback his testimony caused wouldn't be put on Joci or his boys.

For the next few hours, he scoured the video surveillance of Jerry, Bambi, and Joci. Normally he wouldn't mind following his fiancée around, but it made him feel disconnected from the world—from her.

Afterward, he completed the doctor's mandated home therapy. Once he was sweaty, he hopped in the shower, then attempted a nap. He couldn't fall asleep despite barely sleeping over the last weeks. Not having Joci by his side kept him awake. Not knowing if she was safe kept dreams at bay. The anticipation was slowly killing him. *Not to mention being on the outside of everything.*

By the time Quinn rolled around to pick him up, his

nerves were on edge.

"You good?"

Cameron followed him to the elevator and pushed the button. "Yep. Ready to get this done and behind us." He watched the illuminated floor numbers tick by. "I want to go home."

Quinn chuckled and nudged him with his arm. "Man, I never thought I'd hear you say shit like that."

"Yeah, well, you go a few months without the love of your life and let me know how you feel." He brushed a hand over his chest and side-eyed his friend. "I doubt you could last long."

Scratching his chin, Quinn nodded. "Yeah, you're probably right, but I'll never have to know. Well, I hope at least."

They reached the garage floor, and Quinn checked the area before waiving Cameron through. They made good time to the meeting point, the town nightlife muted for a Thursday in Des Moines. When they parked in a dark side alley, Cameron immediately surveyed the area for Del Rossi vehicles. None stuck out, so they headed toward the FBI truck down the street.

Joci sat waiting inside, and Cameron resisted the overpowering urge to wrap her in his arms. There'd be plenty of time for it later.

"Remember, you can cancel this at any time if you want," he said after the agents went over the plan one last time.

She managed a small smile. "No, I'm fine. We need to put Jerry where he belongs." She reached over and squeezed his hands. "Then everyone can be where they belong."

He swallowed hard at the fear evident in her hazel eyes. It wasn't an emotion he ever liked seeing in those beautiful depths. He'd brought her into the mob, and it tore him up that he couldn't get her out. Not by himself.

Quinn attached the pin with a small camera to the lapel of her jacket. It was a justice scale and wouldn't look out of place on her with blue jeans, a short-sleeved red blouse, and long beige coat.

"Can you give us a minute?" he asked when the police officers and FBI agents kept chattering at them.

Everyone cleared the large van filled with surveillance equipment, and Cameron waited until the door shut to fuse his lips to Joci's. Her hands gripped the front of his shirt, a desperate moan escaping her mouth. When he finally eased back enough to catch his breath, he cursed.

"I can't lose you, Joce," he said, cupping her face in his hands. "You're everything I never knew I needed."

"I'm not going anywhere, I promise." She slid her hands up his chest and rested them in his hair. "Stay out of sight, okay? I can't live with you on the run from the mob."

A knock on the side of the van reminded him their time was limited. He kissed her again but resisted completely consuming her like his body demanded. "I'll see you when you're done."

She nodded, but the hesitation in her face wasn't lost on him. She was scared. *Hell, so am I.*

***

Watching in the mirror, Joci applied lip balm to her suddenly dry lips and climbed out of her car. The familiar SUV used by the Del Rossi mob boss sat directly across from her. All she had to do was hand him a few documents and her role would be finished. The Feds would take over after that.

Her steps faltered slightly when Jerry stepped out of his vehicle accompanied by four bodyguards with guns. Bambi came into view by the time Joci stood face-to-face with the mobster. The first time they'd met hadn't done Bambi justice. The woman was spectacular. With blonde hair curled at the ends and designer attire from her head to her toes, no man would reject her. *No wonder she got mad when Cam did.*

She kept her head high, remembering the threat Bambi sent before Cameron was shot. *This ends today.*

Sweat lined her palms, but she fought against showing her nerves. If Jerry sensed a trap, he'd go underground. The last thing anyone wanted was him going dark.

"Joci, you're looking beautiful as ever," Jerry greeted, kissing both her cheeks. He stepped back and looked her up and down. "I wish Cameroni could've lived out his days with you." His eyes clouded. "Fate is not always kind to us."

She stepped back enough so his strong cologne didn't churn her stomach more than it already was. "No, it's not."

"But I suspect you'll find love again." He smiled, though the act was anything but sincere. "Perhaps even with someone you wrote off? An ex-husband, maybe?"

"I don't see that happening." Clearing her throat, she

held out the folder. "Everything is in here. All the dismissals. I managed to get my police contact to agree to hear any future altercations first, so they'll help reduce the number of cases."

One of Jerry's men took the information. He didn't bother to open it before tucking it in the small of his back. According to Cameron's experience with Del Rossi, the documents there would be buried in a vault somewhere. Mobsters kept nearly impeccable paper trails. The Feds rarely found the documents they wanted, so this time, the file had a tracking device lined in the binding. Judging by the way no one bothered to scan it, Del Rossi wouldn't discover their mistake until she was long gone.

"We truly appreciate your assistance, Joci." Jerry grasped her hands and squeezed. "Cameron would've wanted this. He once told me he longed for you to be part of Del Rossi as our in-house attorney. It would've been wonderful to have the family together under one business roof, don't you think?"

Joci bit her tongue until she tasted blood. Her brain screamed to tell him off, but she knew better. Too many lives were at stake for her to get one punch at him. No matter how satisfying it would be to yell at him, she refrained. Instead, she nodded and forced a smile.

"Cameron always saw you as a father figure. I'll be the first to say I was wary, but after all you've done for us, I can't complain." She squeezed his hands twice and noticed his smile turned sad. In her heart, she hoped the man hadn't ordered Cameron's death, but his vile sister instead. Some part of him cared enough for Cameron to repeatedly help him out of harm's way. Surely, he wouldn't send one of his own men to the gallows simply because his sister didn't get her way.

"If Del Rossi runs into any more legal troubles, give me a call." She freed her hands and turned. Her car loomed in the distance, salvation so close she could taste it.

"One last thing," a woman's voice said in the night air.

Cringing, Joci glanced behind her. Bambi had walked past her brother and now stood between them.

"Yes?"

"I didn't get a chance to say goodbye to Cameron the way I wanted." The blonde pushed back her big curls. "Any chance I can visit his grave?"

Joci swallowed the bile rising in her throat. She'd never hit anyone before, but the cocky smile on Bambi's face just might change that.

"Unfortunately, no. We'll be scattering his ashes later this month."

"Pity. I had so many wonderful things to say." Bambi preened and looked down her nose at Joci. "I never thought he'd go for a brunette. Blondes were always his women of choice."

"Guess enough blondes screwed him over that a change was in order," she couldn't help but reply.

Bambi narrowed her gaze, and Jerry stepped in with a chuckle.

"Come, sister. We have other meetings tonight." He nodded to Joci. "We'll be in touch."

She watched them retreat before returning to her car.

Once inside, she let her emotions loose, and her entire body shook uncontrollably. She was amazed she'd held it together so long.

Her breathing finally evened out, and she put the car into gear. She'd make it to the rendezvous point with the FBI, then she'd go back to the Petosa penthouse for the night while the agencies tracked down Jerry. Rayna and the boys were there now, and she couldn't wait to see them. Her little family would be together at long last. They'd survived Del Rossi. If that didn't earn them a vacation, she didn't know what did.

Several FBI agents and Quinn met her at the parking garage. He wrapped her in a hug when she stepped out of the car.

"You did it, Joce. We'll get this son of a bitch for everything." He kissed the top of her head in a brotherly fashion. It was the only way she could see him anymore.

"Good. I'm ready to live without a mafia involved." She looped her arm around his waist, and they caught the elevator down to the skywalk level. Officers were stationed along the downtown area in case Del Rossi followed her.

It took longer than a direct approach to reach the firm, but once they stepped into the front lobby, Joci was grateful for the extra precautions. By now, Cameron was upstairs, and she couldn't wait to be in his arms once more.

Before Quinn could unlock the door to the penthouse, Joci's phone rang. Digging it out of her purse, she held it up. Her eyes widened. "It's Jerry."

Quinn motioned to the FBI agent nearby and pulled a

recording app up on his phone. "Answer it."

"Hello?"

"Joci, I'm glad I caught you. I forgot to invite you to our family dinner on Tuesday night."

"Oh, uh, I'm not family."

He chuckled. "Cameron meant a lot to me. I watched him grow from a skinny kid to a man I'd be proud to call my own. The two of you were meant to be together. I'm glad he had you for a little while."

Tears trickled down Joci's cheeks. "Then why'd you let him die?" she burst out before she could stop.

"I didn't, but I also didn't have control over the situation." He sighed. "Plans go awry sometimes. If I'd been there, I promise you he'd be here today."

She glanced to the penthouse door and saw Cameron in the doorway. His brown eyes were fixed on the phone. Suddenly, it was all clear. Jerry didn't call for Cameron to be shot; Bambi did. He'd all but admitted it just then. They'd guessed, but hearing the words brought it home for her.

"I wish I could believe you, Jerry." She gripped the android a little tighter.

"Well, I know you don't believe anything you can't deduce for yourself, but I do consider you to be family. I failed Cameron. I won't fail you or his children. That much I swear."

"Goodbye, Jerry." She hung up and looked to Quinn. He merely nodded, then stepped away with the small group of officers that had gathered during the conversation.

Her eyes met Cameron's and she fell into his embrace

before any more tears could fall. He smoothed a hand over her hair, slowly pulling her into the apartment.

"He's hard to hate sometimes, isn't he?" he whispered against her head. "Always knows exactly how to seem like a good guy."

She nodded, burrowing further into his arms. "You're the only good guy in this."

He kissed the top of her head. "I don't know about that, but I'm doing my best." He guided her to the door. "C'mon, Rayna's getting the boys ready for bed. We should relieve her."

"Hey, don't fall asleep or anything just yet," Quinn called out. "I need to get statements from both of you."

Joci nodded but didn't hear the rest of what he said. All she wanted to do was curl up next to Cameron and watch their babies sleep. It was all she could handle for the night.

CHAPTER NINETEEN

The next morning, Cameron carefully crept out from beneath the tight grip Joci had on him. It took every bit of willpower to leave her lying there with a sheet as the only covering for her beautiful body. He placed a gentle kiss on the tip of her nose and grabbed the clothes on top of the dresser.

He made it to the hallway and held his breath when the door creaked ever so slightly. Tugging on his shirt and pants, he winced at the pain thanks to the healing gunshot wounds. *Would not recommend getting shot again. Zero stars.* He smirked. Joci would appreciate the humor. *Though, probably not right now.*

Checking on the twins, he grinned at the sight of Levi sucking his thumb and Brett sprawled out on his stomach with his little diapered butt sticking up in the air. He'd do anything for them, including sneaking out to keep them safe.

The sun peeked over the horizon, the sight usually stunning. This morning was different. It only made his stomach ball into one giant knot. Quinn had texted him after Joci fell asleep. Jerry was on the move and the FBI had lost his trail. Someone had found the tracker, and the mobster was on his way underground.

Cameron slipped on his shoes and hastily scribbled a note for Joci to find on the counter by the coffeepot. It was the one place he was certain she'd look. *And it's not like I won't be back in a couple of hours.*

A knock on the door had him hurrying to open it before Joci woke up. He nodded to Quinn and slipped out of the penthouse with one last glance behind him.

"All set?" Quinn asked, handing him a handgun.

Cameron checked the safety and tucked the gun in the small of his back. "Let's shut this bastard down."

***

Two hours passed, and they still waited for Jerry to pop his head out of his hotel bunker. Plenty of Del Rossi men filtered in and out of the residence, an exodus evident in their actions. Cameron couldn't figure out how Jerry had found the tracking device. The FBI had been excruciatingly careful. He'd seen Joci's interactions with Jerry and Bambi and didn't recognize any reason for the mob to suspect foul play. In the end, it didn't matter. Joci and the boys were safe, and he and Quinn would finish this once and for all.

"We've got some movement on the north side," a voice said over Quinn's radio.

"Copy that." Quinn glanced over at him. "Think Jerry's fueling the private jet?"

"I wouldn't expect anything less." Cameron checked his phone and saw a missed call from Joci. He hadn't been really specific in the note, and she probably wanted answers. He pulled up a text exchange and started to type a message when Quinn whistled.

"There he is."

Cameron lifted his gaze and watched his mob boss hurry to the largest SUV in the armada. Two other SUVs sandwiched Jerry's between them and they started north, most likely toward a private airstrip. Jerry preferred the smaller airports to sneak in and out of places.

"Are we following him or what?" He buckled his seat belt and motioned for Quinn to move.

"Unit 7345 in pursuit," Quinn said over the radio.

"Good copy, 7345. Keep a safe distance," the FBI agent replied.

They were doing this by the book even though Cameron suggested the opposite. He wanted Del Rossi gone and didn't care if lines were crossed to make it happen. Smoothing a hand over his black T-shirt, he tucked his phone in his pocket. Joci didn't need a play-by-play. It'd only make her worry. He was safe. That's all he'd texted her. Later, he'd fill in the blanks.

Jerry's vehicles kept at the speed limit, careful not to attract attention. It was obvious the three cars were together. They weaved in and out of traffic like pros, never once giving a car the opportunity to come between them. Quinn kept in the far-right lane on the interstate, the destination clear in everyone's mind. The FBI and DMPD waited at the airport fifteen miles north of Des Moines. They wouldn't strike until Jerry boarded the plane.

Once they reached the interstate exit, Quinn turned down a maintenance road parallel to Jerry's SUVs. Attaining the large hangers, they parked near one of the smaller jets, and Cameron hopped out before Quinn stopped the vehicle.

He drew his gun and kept to the shadows. The clouds overhead let the sun out every now and again, a slight breeze ruffling Cameron's hair. Jerry's barked orders in Italian drifted to him. The mobsters hustled to do their boss's bidding. No one back talked, and it appeared the airplane was nearly ready for takeoff.

Where's Bambi? He reviewed the group, but none were dressed in the bright colors typical of the blonde. An uneasy feeling settled in his gut.

"Jesus, you couldn't wait until I threw it in Park?" Quinn said, catching up to him. His gun was ready for action, his finger resting on the trigger.

"Do you see Bambi around at all?" he asked, ignoring the other question.

Quinn edged toward the side of the maintenance building and peeked around the corner. After a few seconds, he shook his head. "No. That's weird. Jerry doesn't seem like the type of guy who'd leave his sister behind." He grabbed his radio, but Cameron stopped him before he could send out a call.

"She might be on her way. Let's wait for the FBI to make a move. I don't want to spook him."

In the distance, Cameron spotted FBI agents gathering around the area. He held his breath when they stepped out of the shadows and confronted Jerry.

"FBI, everybody down," one of the agents yelled, which

set off Jerry's men. Gunshots zoomed every direction, and Cameron and Quinn quickly entered the firefight. He managed to clip one of Jerry's guys in the shoulder, bringing him down easily. FBI agents wove through the open space, catching Del Rossi members until only Jerry and his immediate bodyguards were left.

Quinn tapped Cameron's shoulder, and they hurried toward where Jerry stood with a condescending smirk on his face.

"Look, if you want to stay back that's totally okay," Quinn said with a concerned glance.

He shook his head and walked toward the mob boss. "I'll be fine."

They reached the epicenter of the standoff, and Cameron felt Jerry's eyes on him. The mobster dropped his gun and started clapping.

"I knew you weren't dead." Jerry preened, meshing his fingers together as if no one but them were there. "Bambi wanted it so badly, but I knew Charlie wouldn't do it. You two have history, right?"

Cameron walked to the edge of the circle around Jerry. "Yeah, I saved his ass one time."

"A debt repaid then." Jerry chuckled and kept eye contact with him. "Well, I'm glad to see you survived. It makes sense that Charlie put a few bullets in you for flair. I guess it also made everyone think the job had been completed."

"Give it up, Jerry. The Feds won't let you walk away this time." He kept a good grip on his gun. There was no way he'd holster it until handcuffs were on the Italian mafia legend.

"You know, I would, but I've never been one to give in."

"Where's Bambi?" Quinn asked. "You wouldn't leave her behind, so where is she?"

"She left yesterday," Jerry replied, glancing to Quinn.

"Bullshit. The police have been tailing you for weeks. Bambi hasn't left the hotel." Quinn squared his shoulders, and Cameron could only assume he was giving Jerry a death glare. "Or has she?"

In Italian, Jerry instructed his men to drop their weapons. The two did so without hassle, and the FBI agents wrestled them to the ground. No one touched Jerry yet. Agent Stevens twirled cuffs from his finger but didn't make the move to snap them in place.

"Bambi had one last errand to run," Jerry finally admitted. His eyes scanned their surroundings. "She didn't want to leave without saying goodbye to our mutual friend, Cameroni."

The air in Cameron's lungs escaped in a swift whoosh. He stomped toward Jerry and punched the mobster in the face. Grabbing his lapels, Cameron forced Jerry to face him. "Joci? Seriously, Jerry? You loved her like a daughter."

Jerry chuckled. "My track record with family isn't too good. You should've realized this by now. I couldn't stop her from demanding your death, just like I couldn't stop her from making her own plans. Bambina promised to meet me in Chicago tomorrow. That's all I know."

"She'll kill them all, Jerry. Everyone I love. Joci, Brett, and Levi." He gritted his teeth at the mere thought. *I never should've left them this morning.*

A trickle of blood pooled on Jerry's chin. "What's a life without the one you love, eh, Shearer? Bambi was merely putting out misery's flame."

"Fucking bastard. You're sick." Pushing him away, Cameron sprinted toward the undercover squad car, stitches be damned. Just as he turned the key, Quinn jumped in the passenger side.

"You don't think I'm coming?" He buckled and patted the console. "Because if Joci's in danger, so is Rayna."

Cameron shifted gears and the screech of tires sounded beneath them. His partner wasn't wrong. Rayna had planned to visit them that morning. If she had, more lives were in danger than they could help.

He flipped on the police lights and siren while Quinn called for backup. Joci could handle herself, but Bambi wasn't a typical woman. He clenched his jaw until it hurt. The odometer needle flew by one hundred, cars whizzing out of their way. They'd get there in time. If they didn't, he'd never forgive himself.

CHAPTER TWENTY

"You're such a big boy, yes, you are," Rayna cooed in a baby voice.

Joci glanced over and saw her best friend nibble on Levi's bare feet. He giggled and squirmed, obviously loving the attention. Brett grabbed the end of her hair and pulled, stealing her gaze again.

"And so are you, silly." She kissed the side of his neck and he clapped excitedly. Finishing up the diapering, Joci settled Brett on her hip and walked over to where Rayna and Levi sat. "You ready to go?"

Rayna's gray eyes lit up. "Yep. We're all set to tackle the grocery store." She lifted Levi's arms to make it look like his was cheering. "Yay, shopping time! Stick with me, kiddos, and we'll buy a ton of toys for you."

Joci smirked and grabbed the diaper bag. Her eyes rested on the note Cameron left. Despite calling and texting him, his only response was saying he was safe. *Yeah, right.* He left and wouldn't answer her calls or texts. He was far from safe.

Being in the dark was never ideal, but particularly when it had to do with Del Rossi. She stuffed her phone in her purse and waited until Rayna gathered Levi to leave the penthouse. The FBI had insisted on two agents being posted outside the door, and she waited until they cleared the elevator to join the silent men, guns ready on their hips.

Rayna and Joci chatted while the agents checked the garage vicinity for danger. Even though she understood the need for their safety, it was more of an inconvenience when two little boys were anything but patient. They stepped into the garage before she received a phone call from their assistant.

"Joci, I need you to sign the subpoenas for the Miller case. The depositions are Monday and they need to be served over the weekend," the woman said.

Groaning, Joci unlocked the car door and settled Brett in his car seat. "Okay, I'll be right up. I'm in the garage, so it'll be a minute before I get there." She shut the door and looked over the top of the Mercedes. "I need to run up to the office really quick. Can you stay with the boys? I shouldn't be too long."

Rayna finished up with Levi and nodded. "You bet. We'll rock out to some kid songs while we wait."

"Thanks!" Rayna climbed in the car, one agent staying with her, and Joci hurried back to the elevator the second FBI agent in tow. "Five minutes in the office. Just what I need." She punched the button for the firm floor and checked her phone. *Nothing new from Cam. Ugh.*

The door sprung open at last, and she quickly signed

the subpoenas at her assistant's desk. "Let me know if the process server can't get these done," she said, walking backward toward the elevator. Her five minutes had turned into ten before she knew it, and she doubted the twins would be good for much longer.

"Joce, you want to get dinner later?" Adrian called from the doorway of his office.

"Yeah, sure." She walked over and lowered her voice and nodded to the less than discreet FBI agent by the elevator. "We're staying at the penthouse tonight again just to be safe." The whole firm didn't always need to know her whereabouts. One could never be too careful.

"All right, I'll pick up sushi then." He smirked. "Unless you want something different?"

"Sushi sounds great." She smiled. "But I need to go. Rayna's downstairs with the boys."

"Grocery time?"

"You know it."

He chuckled. "Good luck."

She nodded and checked the time once she was on the elevator. When the elevator stopped on the lobby level, she glanced to the FBI agent and frowned. *Must be somebody getting on to go to the garage.* She moved to the side in case more than one person hopped on for the short distance. What met her eyes when the door slid open caused her pulse to skyrocket.

"Bambi." Before she uttered the name, the blonde woman cocked her Beretta and let off a shot, the bullet hitting the FBI agent in the head. Blood splattered over Joci's face, and she was too stunned to scream or even move.

"Hello, Joci." Bambi smiled coldly.

Immediately, Joci recognized the outcome. "Look, I should be going." She reached for the button to close the door, but Bambi pointed the gun at her.

"Not so fast, mama. We need to chat." She waved for Joci to follow.

Flashbacks of the last year swarmed her. They would've crippled her movements if the glare in Bambi's blue eyes hadn't summoned her forward. She had to live, and that meant following the rules even if her stomach warned her not to.

"Where's Cameron?" Bambi asked once they were down the hall and tucked into an empty hallway out of sight.

"I don't know what you're talking about," she replied automatically. A fierce pain whipped through Joci's face at the slap of the gun.

"Don't lie to me!" she screamed. "I spoke to every damn funeral home in the area. None of them cremated a body with his name."

Joci reached up and massaged her jaw. Cold blood from the FBI agent met her fingers, and she wiped it off with her dark shirt. "That's because I didn't use his real name."

Bambi narrowed her fake eyelashes. "I don't believe you."

"I don't care." She moved to escape the conversation, but Bambi pointed the gun at Joci's head.

"Move, and I pull the trigger."

"Look, I don't know what you want from me. I'm just

trying to go to the store." Her pulse quickened, and she held down the bile rising in her throat. It'd be too obvious if she reached into her purse and grabbed her cell phone. The little information she knew about Bambi, anything could start the blonde on a shooting spree.

For a long moment, Bambi stared at her. The overpowering scent of her expensive perfume invaded Joci's nostrils, but she refrained from coughing. In order to make it out alive, she needed to stay in control of her emotions. *Even if I want to headbutt her.*

"I understand why he liked you." Bambi traced Joci's face with the tip of the gun. "You aren't like the normal girls who hang around mobs. You're unique." She snorted and snatched Joci's purse, waving the cell phone that could've called for help. "Pathetic. He could've stayed alive, you know? All he had to do was choose me. Well, and a life with Del Rossi. As if the mob would ever let him out without a bullet in his head. In the back of his mind, I think he knew. He didn't cry or beg for his life, if that gives you any closure. He greeted death like a man."

Joci balled her hands into fists. It physically hurt to stay quiet. It just wasn't in her nature. She couldn't determine if Bambi's words were a lie or if the woman was trying to get a reaction. The wail of police sirens echoed from the street, and Joci prayed their destination was the building. If Cameron and Quinn caught wind of Bambi's plan, they'd be on their way.

"Hear that?" Joci nodded to the door. "The police will be here anytime now. You should leave before they get here."

Bambi pressed the gun to Joci's forehead. "Shut up. I'm not going anywhere."

The sound of screeching tires gave Joci fleeting hope. The first place the police would look was the penthouse, then her office. They wouldn't find her tucked away on the lobby floor until it was too late. She wished she could signal the officers somehow.

Bambi's eyes flashed panic when loud voices echoed along the hallway, then combat boots hit the lobby. The police had arrived but didn't know where she was. Holding the barrel of the gun over Joci's lips in silent warning, Bambi waited until the voices subsided to nudge her further down the hall.

"Joce, is everything okay?" Adrian's voice drifted from the end of the hallway.

Her heart surged with renewed hope. She looked behind Bambi and met Adrian's worried eyes. Surely, he'd seen Bambi's gun moments earlier. If not, she'd make it blatantly obvious what the woman was up to. Her shirt was too dark to show the blood, but maybe she'd missed some of it on her face.

"Tell him you're fine or I shoot your babies in front of you," Bambi threatened under her breath. She gripped Joci's left wrist and cozied up against her, facing the opposite direction. She jabbed the gun against Joci's rib cage as a reminder.

Clearing her throat, Joci reached up to make it look like she scratched her right temple. Doing so, she covertly spelled out SOS with her finger. It didn't take Adrian long to figure out the silent call for help. His eyes widened, but he kept his place.

"Yeah, I'm fine. Just chatting with a fellow attorney."

He took a few steps closer. "Oh, yeah? Are you new to the firm?"

Joci silently swore at his idiocy. She could distract Bambi long enough for him to get a security guard. But no, Adrian wasn't the type to run for help. He preferred being the savior himself.

Bambi flashed Joci a warning, then turned on her red heels. No doubt a brilliant smile graced her lips and displayed a row of white teeth. "I actually just stopped by to turn in my résumé."

Adrian's hands remained behind his back, and Joci hoped his phone was there too. One of them had to think of an exit plan. Seeing how Adrian walked right into the hostage situation, it was up to her.

"Wonderful. We can always use new attorneys in the firm. What type of law do you practice?"

"General." Bambi's fake nails dug into Joci's wrist.

"Adrian, can you check on the boys? I left them with Rayna in the garage. I'll call you later, okay?" She widened her eyes and hoped he'd get the hint. He stood next to her now.

Before he could budge, another voice spoke.

"Drop the gun, Bambi."

Joci lunged for an escape, but Bambi grabbed her hair and yanked her back before pressing the gun to her cheek. She yelped in pain, the sound echoing in the empty area.

"I knew it," Bambi scoffed, shaking her head. "The great Cameron Shearer doesn't die so easily."

Glancing at the quickly shrinking area, Joci noticed Quinn close behind her fiancé. Relief should've overwhelmed her, but only nagging guilt filled her. Even though it was two against one where weapons were concerned, she didn't like the odds of a psychopath against cops.

Cameron kept his gun trained on the blonde. "Damn right I don't." He nodded to Joci. "Let her go and we can talk about this."

Bambi let out a high-pitched laugh. "Now, why would I want to do that? I have the one person you love more than yourself at my mercy. I get to watch you suffer while I kill her."

Quinn cocked his gun and took a step closer. "You do, and you die. Let her go, and you'll live."

"Or I could just vanish. After killing her, of course." Bambi pulled her gun away slightly, and Joci took her chance. She quickly bolted away from the mobster.

"Get back here!" Bambi yelled.

"Adrian, let's go," Joci called, grabbing his wrist.

Quinn and Cameron continued to yell at Bambi, both promising to take her down if she moved an inch. The loud pop of a gun exploded in the havoc, silencing Joci's mind momentarily. All she could hear was the whizzing of the bullet and the ripping flesh when it hit muscle.

A round of shots peppered the space, this time hitting their mark in Bambi Del Rossi. Joci watched the blonde slump to the ground, blood staining the white marble floor.

She closed her eyes, expecting the inevitable pain in her chest. When it didn't come, she looked up to see Adrian's body directly in front of hers. He staggered on his feet, reaching for anything to hold him up. His eyes latched on to her, and he let out a gasp.

"Oh my God, Adrian!" Joci caught him before he fell, though all she really did was help him to a softer landing. She wasn't strong enough to hold up his full weight. A dark stain crept over his shirt, destroying the expensive material.

Carefully, she sank to the floor with his head in her lap. His lips moved wordlessly, and tears immediately flooded her eyes.

"Shh, it's going to be okay. We'll get you to the hospital." She took one of his hands and pressed it against her lips.

"I don't think so this time." He reached up and tugged on a strand of her hair. His eyes searched her face, his blue eyes full of unshed tears. One escaped, and she shook her head.

"No, don't give up, Adrian. Please." She wiped away his tears, her own falling on his face.

On the edge of reality, she heard Quinn call the paramedics to the lobby. Cameron ripped off his shirt and pressed it against the wound to stop the bleeding. The crimson liquid soaked straight through despite the pressure.

"Guess somebody finally broke my heart, huh?" He chuckled and winced.

"Stop talking like that. The paramedics will be here any minute, and they'll—"

"Joce, please don't." He shook his head. "I've done a lot of bad things during my life, but I never regretted you.

Loving you was the best thing I ever did. I'm sorry for the pain I put you through. You never deserved any of it." His bottom lip quivered, and more tears dripped to his cheeks. "Take care of our boy, okay? He's going to be a handful when he's older, if he's anything like me."

"I will, but—"

"And Cam...." Adrian stole Cameron's hand from pressing against the wound. "Take care of her."

Cameron looked to Joci, then back to Adrian. "You have my word."

Adrian chuckled. "I heard once that you shouldn't take the word of a mobster."

"Then it's a good thing I'm not one anymore." He squeezed Adrian's hand. "Well, that's a relief." Adrian winced when Cameron quickly returned to his attempts to save him. He focused on her, searching her face. "Joce, everything is yours."

"What?"

"The firm, my accounts, everything." Adrian smiled, his face already whiter than normal. "They've always been yours. I never removed you as beneficiary. It was always you."

"Adrian." She shook her head and cupped his face. "You're a good man. No matter what you did in the past, you are someone Brett will be proud to call his dad."

His breathing waned. "I love you, Joci."

Joci could barely see through her teary eyes. "I love you too."

He smiled one last time before his eyelids closed and his

body went slack.

Cameron checked Adrian's pulse. "I'm sorry, Joci. He's gone."

Her vision blurred completely then. Her devastation was for their son. She cared about him and loved him as Brett's father, but her grief held no other meaning. She'd mourned him once and she thought it'd be the only time.

Her heart heaved at the thought of a life without Adrian in it. They'd rebuilt a friendship over the last months and now he was gone permanently. *He sacrificed his life for mine.* She couldn't think of a better reason to love someone.

Voices filled the lobby and the hallway. The backup police and the paramedics finally reached them. Just too late. She looked over to Cameron and saw his cheeks were wet.

Leaning down, she pressed a kiss to Adrian's forehead. The paramedics took his body away after that. She could hardly remember how it all happened. One moment, Adrian was bleeding out on her and the next she was cold, so very cold.

Cameron wrapped her in his embrace and she clung to his shoulders. Heavy tears coursed down her face as she watched Adrian disappear into a body bag.

"We're going to be okay," he said against her head.

Looking up, she managed a nod. "I know. You're all I need."

Rays of sunshine warmed the arm Cameron hung out the window as he rode shotgun in the police SUV. The summer was nearly over, and plenty had happened over the humid months. He glanced over to Quinn and smirked. The guy never changed. It was part of why they got along. Quinn was by the book in just about everything, but every now and then, he'd skirt those lines of right and wrong. It's why their partnership was perfect.

Despite being in protective custody, Jerry Del Rossi had been murdered before his first court appearance. Some suspected his own brothers had the job done to keep secrets under wraps. Out of the three brothers, Jerry was the weakest link. For a short time, Cameron felt bad for the mobster.

Before the end, Jerry had sworn to never tell anyone of Cameron's betrayal. From what Cameron gleaned from his informants, his name had been wiped from Del Rossi completely. It was partly why he believed Jerry's demise was at the hands of his brothers. Jerry would do anything to save his own ass. If it meant serving up a few people in the process, he'd do it.

Cameron watched the cars brake hard as their vehicle sped by. The job would never get old in his opinion. Then again, he really hadn't been at it long.

"You think Joci will like your surprise?" Quinn asked, breaking into Cameron's thoughts.

"Hell yeah. What girl doesn't like tickets to her favorite band?" He pulled out the second-row tickets from his pocket. That wasn't the full surprise, but she'd get the rest later. Thanks to being a crucial player involved in taking down the Del Rossi mob in Des Moines, the police chief had given him a promotion. It paled in comparison to the money he'd made as a mobster, but this felt better. More fulfilling. Joci would be proud of his detective status. He never doubted it for a minute.

He eyed Quinn. "Think Rayna will be excited for you?"

"Of course." Quinn preened. He'd also been dubbed a detective, and their time of buddying up in the patrol car would soon come to an end. In a way, Cameron thought it was necessary. Their lives were already mingled thanks to the women they loved.

He turned toward the airport, and Cameron cocked his eyebrow.

"Where're we going? I thought we were heading back to the station."

"Just have to check on something here," Quinn said slyly. "Got a tip I thought we should follow up on."

Cameron's phone buzzed, and seeing Joci's name, he answered it. "Hey, babe."

"Hey."

"What's up?"

"Is your passport still in the box under our bed?"

He glanced over to Quinn, but the other man didn't seem to hear the conversation. "Um, yeah, why?"

"No reason. I gotta run. Love you!"

"Yeah, love you too." He hung up and shook his head. Just when he thought he knew Joci, she surprised him. It was one of the many reasons he fell for her each and every day.

Ten minutes later, they pulled up to the airport. He grabbed the laptop, ready to catch up on reports, but Quinn cleared his throat.

"All right, come on. I need your help with this one." He smirked and parked the SUV in front of one of the sliding doors.

He glanced at the airport, then gave him a curious look. "Fine, but you're buying the first round of drinks tonight."

Quinn chuckled and shook his head. "Sure, whatever you say."

As they walked toward the doors, Cameron realized exactly why his partner laughed. He wouldn't be making happy hour tonight.

***

Joci double-checked the itinerary for the surprise trip. Everything was booked and ready to go. Even the plane was nearly ready to board, and she hoped Quinn wouldn't be late. She wasn't about to leave the other half of her honeymoon package in Iowa. Not when St. Lucia was involved.

Brett's laugh echoed near the airport bookstore, making her smile. Traveling with children wasn't something she'd ever dreamed she'd do, but she couldn't leave them at home. Peeking around the corner, she caught sight of the new nanny they'd hired at the beginning of the summer. The woman in her thirties was perfect for their family. From the conversations they'd had over the months, Joci didn't expect Svetlana to ever leave them either.

Her phone rang, and she quickly answered. "Did you get it?"

"Yep. On my way now. Any chance I can get a police escort so I can speed?" Rayna teased from the other end.

Joci smirked. "You're beginning to sound like Quinn."

"Ugh, now that would be a disaster."

"Would it, Ray?" She slowly paced in front of the wall of windows facing the airport drop-off area. "Because I'm fairly certain Quinn wouldn't mind one bit."

She could almost hear the sound of Rayna's gray eyes rolling.

"You know I don't like to be tied down, Joce. Wild and free and all that jazz."

"Mm-hmm. Well, don't be surprised if Quinn changes your mind."

Rayna snorted. "Even if I wanted Quinn in the long run, I don't think I could ever be a cop's wife. Too much stress involved."

Instead of arguing, Joci shook her head and said, "Whatever you decide is fine with me. I want you to be happy."

"Of course the person about to jet off to somewhere tropical says that."

"You're coming too, Rayna, remember?" She glanced to the carry-on luggage near the nanny. "Or should I just donate your stuff to one of these nice travelers?"

"I'll be there in five."

Hanging up, she walked over and gave Levi a kiss on his little nose. The boys were growing faster than she was ready for. They were walking everywhere and getting into trouble just as often.

Svetlana zoomed Brett like an airplane around the waiting area, and the redheaded boy squealed with delight. His bright blue eyes met Joci's, and she caught her breath. He looked identical to Adrian. There were parts of her too, but when she looked into his face, Adrian was there.

A tinge of sadness crept into her mind. Losing Adrian a second time wasn't any easier than the first. In fact, in many ways, she found it harder. While she didn't love him in a romantic sense, she'd grown to care for him as Brett's father and as a friend. He'd paid the ultimate price for her safety, and she'd forever be grateful to him for that. Little Brett would always know who his biological father was and what he'd done for their family. Cameron supported the decision wholeheartedly from day one.

An email dinged on her phone. She scanned the reminder from the Petosa board of directors but didn't bother to reply. Adrian had left everything to her, including Petosa Law. As much as she appreciated the gesture, she didn't want to control the large firm. She maintained a seat on the board, but that was it. She'd officially resigned as an attorney on their roster so she could focus on the firm with Rayna. Money wasn't something to worry about, thanks to Brett Sr. and Adrian, but despite the inheritances, she continued her work as an attorney at the office she'd built with Rayna. Life wasn't the same without the law involved.

"Joce, I just saw them pull up," Rayna said excitedly, suddenly beside her. She hadn't even heard the other woman approach.

"Thanks." She grabbed Cameron's passport and walked over to the entrance. Somehow she abstained from shouting to Cameron when he hopped out of the squad car.

He strode toward the automatic doors, his swagger unlike any other man's. Even though he wasn't the bad boy she'd met again nearly three years ago, she couldn't see herself loving him more. But she would. Loving Cameron came in waves, each always stronger than the last. He could be a hobo and she'd love him. The perks of his job only added to his badass persona.

The dark police uniform hugged his muscles as he walked, every now and then saying something to his partner. Seeing how promotions had to be on the horizon after the Del Rossi takedown, their partnership wouldn't last forever. She was all right with that. It'd give her more chances to visit him at work without Quinn interrupting them.

Her pulse sped up when his brown eyes looked her way. They melted her into a puddle and would continue that tradition until her last breath. He was the man meant for her. She never really believed in fate, but he made her think differently. Their love had fought through the toughest of situations until their lives were exonerated. And now, she stood in black flip-flops, a pair of denim shorts, and a white V-neck tank top with her sunglasses hooked to the front, waiting for the love she always knew existed. Credence was what she strived for in law, and now in love, she'd found it.

"Hey, Counselor, what's going on?" Cameron asked, stepping over the threshold and into the airport. He glanced to Quinn beside him, and the other man chuckled. His eyes scanned her body. "Damn, you look good."

Heat flooded her cheeks. His voice never ceased to seduce her. "I thought maybe we could go on a trip."

His left brow quirked up, and a boyish grin covered his face. "Oh, yeah? For what?"

"To make you my husband."

For one split second, Cameron didn't move. His eyes were glued to hers, endlessly searching.

"We don't have to go anywhere for you to do that, babe," he said, taking a step closer. He pushed the braid off her shoulder, and she shivered when his fingers traced the tank top strap. It happened any time he touched her. He may caress her skin, but he was actually touching her soul.

"No, we don't. But I thought we could take a little vacation afterward." She waved his passport and bit her bottom lip. "What do you think? Just you, me, our boys, and our best friends on a beach."

He wrapped his arms around her and lifted her off the floor, kissing her as his answer. Joci's mind spun at the possibilities that lay within his arms. They were endless.

Just like her feelings for him.

"I can't think of anything better," he finally said, placing her back on solid ground.

Neither could she. Life with Cameron wasn't a fairy tale—*because obviously those don't exist*—but it was real and all she needed.

***

Married. It sounded as weird to his ears as Cameron thought it would. But in the best possible way. Surrounded by sand, sea, tropical gardens, and the people he called family, he recited vows he'd worked on during the plane ride from Iowa.

As the tide rolled in and covered his toes, it didn't feel real. For a man who'd once sworn off anything but the mob, it would take some time to accept. *I guess I did get my happily ever after.* It happened on its own and before he could recognize it.

Reggae music drifted to him, and he looked over his shoulder. Their small wedding group danced in the cove lit with white paper lanterns. The best view, though, was Joci. True to her unique self, her wedding dress was anything but bland. The gown hit just below her knees and the blue ombre train flowed behind her. Fashion wasn't his forte, but he'd bet his savings that she rocked the sweetheart strapless dress better than a model could. Her hair was loosely curled and flowed in the tropical breeze.

She caught him ogling and made her way toward him. The sight was sheer perfection with the sun setting behind her.

He never believed in angels until their paths crossed. He smirked. *Well, if angels are fiery and feisty.*

"What're you doing way out here by yourself?" she asked, her hands propped on her hips. "And on your wedding day, no less."

Cameron chuckled and looped an arm around her shoulder, pulling her close. The scent of coconuts and berries was only outdone by the coffee somehow lingering on her skin. It was Joci to a tee.

"Just needed a quick breath of air." He kissed her temple. "Having a good time?"

She cozied closer into his crisp white shirt. He'd never have guessed she'd want him informal for their wedding but didn't argue when a white button-up and gray pants were delivered along with a blue bow tie that matched the hue of the dress's ombre.

"I always have a good time with you." She kissed his jaw with just a hint of whiskers. "Unless a mob is involved."

"Or an ex."

She looked up at him and teased, "Or a hot cop booty call."

He laughed and cupped her face. "Yeah, any of those. Although, I'm fairly certain you were still having a good time with me despite those distractions." He placed a light kiss to her lips. "I did win, after all."

A spark of defiance lit her hazel eyes. "It was a competition, was it?"

"Nah. You loved me from the beginning."

Before she could give another sassy remark, Cameron

encompassed her lips with his and didn't relent until she let out a pleasurable sigh. Pulling back, he pinched his arm just to make sure he wasn't dreaming. That the woman in his arms was his and nobody would take her away again. When she gently pulled on one of his curls, he knew without a doubt he was wide awake.

"Yo, newlyweds, can you stop sucking face for like five seconds?" Quinn heckled, heading their direction with Rayna in tow.

"Damn, I knew I shouldn't have invited them," Joci grumbled good-naturedly.

Cameron grinned and kept Joci safely in his embrace. "What's up?"

"This came for you a few minutes ago." Rayna held out an envelope.

"Who's it from?" Joci asked, opening it. She pulled out a thick card, and Cameron read the contents from over her shoulder.

"*Auguri, Cameroni,*" he read aloud. "Good luck."

"Wait, that's Italian, right?" Quinn asked, his green eyes suddenly alert and glancing around the beach. "As in the language Jerry Del Rossi taught you?"

He shook his head. "That's impossible. Jerry died."

Joci scanned the card again and started laughing. She laughed until tears rolled down her cheeks. Finally, she said, "You should know by now, no one ever dies when they're in the mob."

He shook his head and couldn't help but join her. It was just like Jerry to pull this type of stunt. Hell, it probably wasn't even from the man.

"I think they've had a little too much rum and sun," Rayna said, touching Joci's forehead.

"I'm fine," Joci promised. "Totally fine." She hugged her friend. "Go enjoy your time away, Ray." She hugged Quinn next. "And you too. Go have some naughty fun."

Quinn and Rayna left them after another round of *congratulations* and Cameron was never more grateful for the serenity.

They watched the waves roll in, tickling their bare toes when they least suspected it.

"So, what do we do now, Mr. Shearer?"

The last of the sun dipped below the horizon behind her and Cameron shifted his gaze. "I'd like to say we live happily ever after, but you don't believe in that."

Joci laced her fingers behind his neck and pulled him to her. "I don't usually, but I'll make an exception. You are the one who made me believe in it after all."

"Good because we're going to do exactly that."

Her soft lips met his before he could utter another word. If they didn't ever leave the cocoon of this tropical bliss, he'd be satisfied. And yet, there was something equally as compelling about navigating life with the gorgeous woman beside him.

They'd defied every odd to be together. A mob brought them together and even murder couldn't tear them apart. They were the exception—Joci was his exception—and he planned on never giving her the opportunity to regret it.

"Come on, Counselor, I have a very important date that

includes you, me, and nothing in between." He swooped her into his arms and started toward their bungalow near the beach.

"I'm all for it, but I have one condition," she said seriously.

Pausing at the threshold, Cameron cocked his head to the right. "And what might that be?"

"You call me by my married name."

"But I thought…." A smile spread across his lips when she merely pushed up her glasses and nodded. He didn't need any more incentive.

Kicking the door open, he walked inside. "Anything for you, Mrs. Finally Shearer."

THE END

Thanks for reading *Credence*. I do hope you enjoyed my trilogy. I appreciate your help in spreading the word, including telling a friend. Before you go, it would mean so much to me if you would take a few minutes to write a review and share how you feel about my story so others may find my work. Reviews really do help readers find books. Please leave a review on your favorite book site.

DON'T MISS OUT ON NEW RELEASES, EXCLUSIVE GIVEAWAYS AND MUCH MORE!

JOIN MY NEWSLETTER:

WWW.SKYEMCNEIL.COM

LIKE ME ON FACEBOOK:_

WWW.FACEBOOK.COM/SKYESTHELIMITWRITING

JOIN MY READER GROUP:

WWW.FACEBOOK.COM/GROUPS/287389708375366

FOLLOW ME ON TWITTER:

TWITTER.COM/SKYE_MCNEIL7

FOLLOW ME ON PINTEREST:_

WWW.PINTEREST.COM/SKYEMCNEIL

Thank you to Hot Tree Publishing for taking a chance on The Mobster Files. It's been a wonderful journey and I wouldn't choose anyone else to take it with. I also want to thank my beta readers and editors for pushing me to become a better writer. Of course, I have to thank BookSmith Design for making each Mobster File cover drool-worthy.

Multitudes of thanks to my faithful readers and friends who have supported me from day one.

ABOUT THE PUBLISHER

Hot Tree Publishing opened its doors in 2015 with an aspiration to bring quality fiction to the world of readers. With the initial focus on romance and a wide spread of romance subgenres, we have since opened Tangled Tree Publishing, our crime, thriller, and suspense imprint.

Firmly seated in the industry as a leading editing provider to independent authors and small publishing houses, Hot Tree Publishing is the sister company to Hot Tree Editing, founded in 2012. Having established in-house editing and promotions, plus having a well-respected market presence, Hot Tree Publishing endeavors to be a leader in bringing quality stories to the world of readers.

Interested in discovering more amazing reads brought to you by Hot Tree Publishing? Head over to the website for information:

WWW.HOTTREEPUBLISHING.COM